THE STONEBRIDGE MYSTERIES

-4-

THE CASE OF THE MISSING FIREFLY

CHRIS MCDONALD

**RED DOG
UK**

Published by RED DOG PRESS 2021

First Edition

Hardback ISBN 978-1-914480-49-2
Paperback ISBN 978-1-914480-50-8
Ebook ISBN 978-1-914480-08-9

www.reddogpress.co.uk

Stonebridge Radio Hallowe'en Party

You are cordially invited to the
Stonebridge Radio Annual Hallowe'en Bash
on Winkle Isle.

Comprising a sumptuous meal.
A few scares and an evening of Murder Mystery.

I do hope you can join us.

A. Fernsby

RSVP by 6th October to guarantee your place.
No cost.

1

NO MONEY, MORE PROBLEMS

ALBERT FERNSBY RUBBED his weary eyes and reached for the tumbler that sat on his office desk.

It used to be he'd only drink on special occasions. Then, there'd been a few years where he'd elevated minor wins to full blown celebrations, just so that he could justify the heft of a full glass in his hand. Now, it had become a nightly thing. A glass of wine with dinner. A few fingers of whiskey while he worked in the evening. Sometimes, even a small glass of port before bed.

He was sure Margaret had noticed, but if she had, she hadn't said anything. It wasn't like he was doing it solely in the confines of his office.

It was hard to keep secrets after more than forty years of marriage, and he was hoping that she might see the drinking as a cry for help, rather than for what it actually was—a distraction.

He strained his ears and heard her padding around upstairs, the floorboards creaking under her feet in the bedroom.

He listened for a few more seconds and, when he was happy that he wouldn't be disturbed, pulled out the blue folder from the filing cabinet.

It was innocuous enough. It looked like the dozens of other files and folders in his office, the ones that lined the shelves and held evidence of his business prowess. Receipts of advertising deals and good decisions made at the right time.

The blue file in his hand showed exactly the opposite.

He set the folder in front of him, front and centre on his desk. He glared at it with contempt and thought that a steaming pile of fresh cow dung would be more welcome on his desk than *this*.

Perhaps it was his advancing years or perhaps it was the changing world, he didn't know, but the past year had been a ruinous one. Financially.

Running a radio station was hard work.

Running a local radio station was even harder.

Stonebridge Radio had started with his father all those years ago. Albert looked at the framed pictures on the walls of his office and smiled. The muscles in his face protested; it had been a while since they'd been pulled into this unfamiliar position.

He took in the black-and-white photos of his father, of the newly founded radio station, of presenters who had started small and either gone on to great things in the capital or faded into the obscurity that stacking supermarket shelves offers.

His smile faded at the more recent photos. He knew that he had taken the radio station as far as it could go. The rise of social media, streaming services, podcasting and a certain fruity corporation had been the death knell of local radio.

The businesses who had once relied on the radio for advertising spots had found other means of reaching their customers; viral videos and celebrity endorsements rendering the advertising service at the station all but useless.

Income had fallen and outgoings had risen, and now they were on the brink. The loan repayment letters and the overdraft statements in the folder were testament to that.

He puffed out his cheeks and took a sip of the amber liquid in his glass. It smarted as it dripped down his throat; the cheap supermarket stuff nowhere near as smooth as his favoured brand. A brand that was beyond his means, at the moment.

Beggars can't be choosers.

He rubbed a hand over a couple of days of stubble and sighed.

He'd have to come clean to his wife. She deserved to know that they were having financial difficulties. He knew they were a team and that whatever happened to them, they'd face it together.

Still, admitting defeat was a bitter pill to swallow.

He sighed again as it became clear what he'd have to do. What he'd been trying to circumnavigate for the past few months but now, there was no other option.

The station would have to close.

He thought of his staff—of the lives he'd be throwing into turmoil with his decision. He thought of his poor father, and what he'd think if he were alive to see it.

He was so caught up in his thoughts, that he didn't hear his office door open. He jumped as he caught sight of his wife's recently dyed locks in the doorway.

'Are you alright?' she asked.

'The best,' he smiled.

He watched as her gaze fell first on the almost empty glass and then on the open file. She was a perceptive woman, and a kind one. Instead of commenting, she simply nodded.

'How's your leg feeling today?' she asked.

'A bit better,' he replied.

Albert had lost the bottom half of his right leg in a car accident a few years back. Learning to walk with the aid of a prosthetic limb had been hard on him, his pride dented with each pitying look he'd received. Last night, he'd complained about the stump rubbing. When she'd tended to it, it had been bright red and bleeding a little.

'Can I do anything for you?' she asked.

He shook his head, forced a smile.

'I'll leave you to it then, love. Are you all packed for the weekend?'

Albert sighed.

'I'll take that as a no,' she laughed.

'To be honest, I could do without it.'

'The annual Stonebridge Radio Bash used to be your favourite weekend of the year,' she replied.

'I'm an old man now. I like my own bed, my home comforts.'

'Well, *I'm* looking forward to it,' she said. 'You never know when it's your last one. And, I've always fancied a murder mystery evening—I'm good at guessing the bad guys when we watch Death in Paradise. I think I'll be a dab hand at being a detective. It'll be a laugh.'

Not with the bombshell I'm going to drop, Albert thought to himself.

2

ONTO THE ISLAND

THE WAVES SMASHED against the hull of the boat, slamming it this way and that. The hum of the engine was lost to the howling winds and the captain, when his voice sounded over the public address system, sounded panicked, though he tried to reassure those on board that they were almost at their destination.

Adam Whyte was furious. Not many things scared him (aside from clowns, the thought of a snake slithering up his toilet bowl while he was sat on it, being made into a meme, and the way daddy long legs buzzed around aimlessly while possessing the deadliest poison known to man), but the sea was truly frightening. The vastness of it, the fearsome sharks that lurked beneath the surface and the fact it had swallowed up a ship once deemed "unsinkable" were only a few of the factors that caused this fear.

He and his best friend, Colin McLaughlin, were sat near the back of the boat. Adam was gazing out the window, though he couldn't make out anything except a few twinkling stars that had broken through the blanket of cloud. He certainly couldn't see the island they were heading for.

'Remind me again why I'm here,' he said, turning to Colin.

'Because my mum is paying us both a hundred quid to set up a projector when we get there because her usual tech guy called in sick,' he replied.

Adam thought back to the proposition put to him a few days ago. At the time it had seemed like easy money—one hundred quid for a few minutes work certainly wasn't to be sniffed at. The fact that they had to stay on an island for two nights didn't bother him either, once he'd been assured there was WiFi. He could easily while away the weekend in the company of Cumberbatch and Freeman.

Of course, what hadn't been mentioned was the group of people he'd be having to share a boat ride with.

Colin's mum was an event co-ordinator and had been hired by the Stonebridge Radio team to organise a murder mystery night on Winkle Isle, a small island just off the coast of Stonebridge. Legend had it that the island was the most haunted place in Northern Ireland, which made it the perfect place to host such an event with a Hallowe'en theme.

Had Adam known about the group he'd been sharing the weekend with, he'd have declined instantly.

The Stonebridge Radio presenters were notorious in the area for their childish behaviour, pig-headedness and their absolute willing to do whatever it took to bag the best show. They'd gladly push a colleague in front of a bus if it meant they could climb a rung on the ladder towards the prime-time evening slot; a position currently held by Keith Starr.

At least the owner of the station, Albert Fernsby, was there too, Adam thought. Surely the presenters would be on their best behaviour if the man who paid their wages was on the island too.

'Right,' shouted Drive Time Dave above the cacophony of wind, waves and rain. 'As it's Halloween and everyone has put in a load of effort with their costumes... except for the boss...'

This raised a few sniggers, but not many.

'Here is my proposition,' he continued. 'For the entire weekend, you must keep your outfit on. That means, for the entirety of the time on the island, I will resemble Dracula. The first person to break this rule, will have to pay the drinks tab on Sunday night, and let's face it, that's going to be a bloody fortune! What do we say?'

Not wanting to appear like stick in the muds, the other presenters instantly held aloft a bottle of beer each and agreed.

'This is going to be so much fun,' squealed afternoon presenter Sophie Saunders, who was dressed as a sexy cat.

Adam stared at her. It always amazed him that some people, like her, saw Hallowe'en as an excuse to wear as little as possible. A year ago, his tongue would've been lolling on the floor at the sight of her low-cut top and sheer leggings, but not this year. The newly matured, spoken-for Adam Whyte was more worried about her catching hypothermia on this cold October night.

Adam noticed the other presenters didn't look as enthusiastic as Sophie. Keith Starr, dressed as a fat David Bowie, looked over at Gavin Callaway. Gavin was well over six feet tall, built like a tank and was currently squeezed into black spandex in an effort to look like a 90s wrestler. Gavin rolled his eyes. Keith did too.

Adam turned back to Colin.

'You're a dick for not mentioning who we were coming with.'

'Like it matters,' Colin shrugged. 'It's not like we're going to have to spend any time with them. We set up the projector in the main room and that's the last we see of them.'

'You'd best have brought good snacks.'

Colin zipped open his rucksack to reveal a treasure trove of sugary treats.

'By the end of the weekend, you'll be well on your way to having diabetes.'

'Good man,' laughed Adam, patting his friend on the back.

'You know,' Colin said, 'I was surprised when you agreed to come, if I'm honest.'

'Why?'

'Well, the island has this reputation as being the most haunted place in Northern Ireland…'

'And…?' Adam interrupted.

'Well, you're a bit of a scaredy cat, aren't you? You don't like blood, can't even watch it on telly without feeling faint, and as for horror movies…'

'I just don't see the fun in watching something designed to scare you. It's stupid. And there won't be any of that this weekend. You said it yourself—most of the weekend will be spent in a room, away from whatever it is these idiots get up to.'

Adam was still pontificating about how brave he was as the boat slowed and began to approach the wooden jetty that jutted out from a rocky alcove. The boat rotated and the engine died. There was some shouting as the captain communicated with one of the crew, who had leapt from the boat to the jetty to secure the vessel to land with a length of rope.

The gentle chatter of the guests was interrupted by a guttural scream from outside.

Sophie grabbed hold of Drive Time Dave's arm and Keith jumped a foot in the air, which was a surprising feat considering his girth.

As Adam adjusted himself to try and see what had happened, a sneering moustached face appeared in the circular porthole, almost nose to nose with him. Adam fell off the bench seat onto the floor, pain shooting up his back as his tailbone collided with the hard sole of the ship.

Swear words Colin had never heard before spilled out of his friend's mouth at a rate of knots, as the face disappeared from the window and the body it belonged to started to descend the steps at the front of the boat.

'So,' the tall man said, staring intently at each person in turn, 'you are the island's next victims, hmm?'

Before panic could descend, the tall man broke into a huge smile.

'Sorry about the drama,' he said, his eyes on Adam who was still lying on the floor. 'I am your host for the weekend, and I do like to make a theatrical entrance. Though we've never had someone actually collapse before.'

The guests all turned to where the tall man was looking. Adam's cheeks began to burn as the atmosphere changed. Laughter broke out at the scared young man. One of the DJs actually had tears rolling down his face.

'This is going to be fun,' shouted the tall man.

'This is going to be a bloody nightmare,' thought Adam.

3

THE OMEN

THE TALL MAN stood on the jetty, helping people off the boat and on to dry land. When Adam reached the front of the queue, he eyed the man with mistrust.

'Sorry about before, I didn't mean to frighten you,' the man said.

Adam scoffed.

'You didn't frighten me, you surprised me. There's a difference.'

'If you say so,' smiled the man.

He gripped Adam's hand tightly and pulled him onto the jetty, before moving onto the remaining passengers. As Colin and Adam marched off the rickety, wooden dock, they passed the crew member of the boat who had been tasked with securing the boat with the rope.

'Was it you that did the fake scream?' Adam asked.

'Yep,' the man confirmed, looking pleased with his part in the ruse.

'You're a prick,' said Adam, before walking away.

THE PATH THAT led up to the accommodation was stony and steep. Rain had started to fall not long ago and already the stones were slick and slippery. Up ahead of Adam and Colin, Sophie was begging one of the other presenters to give her a piggy back, as the high heels she had opted for were unsurprisingly ill fitting for the rugged terrain.

A moan of discomfort from behind caused Adam to turn. Albert, who must've been in his mid-sixties, was struggling to climb the hill.

'You need a hand?' Adam said, pointing to his case.

'That'd be very kind,' Albert replied, pointing to his right leg. 'It's this bloody thing, the prosthetic leg. I was in a car crash a few years ago and they had to amputate the bugger. Now, anything that isn't flat makes it feel like I'm climbing bloody Everest.'

Adam didn't want to pry, so took hold of the case wordlessly and dragged it onwards. Colin grabbed hold of Albert's wife's case without asking, for which she thanked him through chattering teeth. They walked a few more steps, when, from nowhere, the tall man appeared, hooking his arm around Adam's neck.

'For f...' Adam started, his heart leaping into his throat. 'Is there any chance that you could cough or something before you give me a bloody heart attack.'

'Sorry about that, I thought you'd seen me.'

'Well, I hadn't. What do you want?'

'Charming,' the tall man said, with a chuckle. 'I thought I'd introduce myself. That way, perhaps you won't have such a fear of me. My name is Damien, and it's lovely to meet you.'

'Damien? Are you being serious?'

'Maybe,' he said, conspiratorially, as he unhooked his arm and hurried on to the next group. Adam heard a swear word uttered in a deep voice from ahead of them. Clearly, Damien's presence had caught them by surprise too.

'Make sure you lock your door tonight,' Adam said to Colin. 'I'd bet you a hundred quid that at some point, that sneaky son of the devil will be standing over your bed with an axe in his hand.'

AT THE TOP of the hill was a narrow path that was presided over by gnarled trees. Trees that had probably been there for centuries and had endured storm after storm, unshielded from the lashing rain and wind. They were stooped over and made Adam feel claustrophobic as he passed under them. He was on edge. All he could think about was how Damien was probably stood behind one of the deformed trunks, waiting for him to pass so that he could scare him once more.

They reached the end of the path without incident. Emerging from the darkness, the group were presented with their lodgings. And they weren't too shabby at all.

It looked to Adam like a small castle. The thick cobblestone walls were illuminated by a number of uplights resting on the grass to the side of the building. Four turrets, at each corner of the square building, disappeared into the rapidly descending darkness and a gravel path bisected the gardens, leading to a pair of heavy oak doors. The rain was really starting to hammer down now, and the group rushed as fast as they could to the entrance. Adam felt sorry for the old man and his wife, who lagged behind. He could hear them bickering, their whispered words carried on the wind.

'Looks like there's a storm brewing,' said Damien, when they were all safely ensconced inside the entrance hall. As if to emphasize his point, a peal of thunder boomed in the distance.

'I'm soaked through,' said the man dressed as a wrestler.

'You're not going to take your outfit off though, are you?' asked Drive Time Dave.

'I don't want to pay for a weekend of booze, so no,' Gavin said. 'I'd rather get hypothermia.'

Damien led them through an impressive foyer, with a black and white tiled floor and expensively framed oil paintings hanging on the walls, into a cosy lounge. A roaring fire was being stoked by a man in a waistcoat, who Adam assumed worked here. The presenters swarmed around the warmth; hands held outstretched to the flames. Albert and his wife sank into a couple of upholstered armchairs, pleased for a moment of respite.

'Are you the technology experts?' the waistcoated man asked.

Colin told them that they were and he led them into a room that had been made up like a wedding function room. A long table was placed along one side of the room, laid with a crisp white table cloth and heavy silver cutlery. Ornate candlesticks were placed at intervals along the table, their flames flickering in the light draught that blew through the room.

A bar with a heavy oak counter top in the corner of the room was being cleaned by a woman in a white blouse, while a man was changing one of the optics affixed to the back wall.

A large, rectangular portion of the room was dedicated to what looked like a dancefloor. A rig of brightly coloured lights had been set up, and a makeshift DJ booth had been assembled and pushed to the side of the room. Beside this, was the equipment that Adam and Colin needed.

They hunkered down and got to work. Adam shoved plugs into sockets and cables into ports. The whirr of the projector coming to life sounded as Colin pulled the canvas down, creating the screen. They adjusted the focus and after five minutes, their job was done.

"Easiest hundred quid I've ever made,' Adam said, as they tidied up the cardboard boxes and hid them behind a long, velvet curtain.

They picked up their sopping backpacks and asked the waistcoated man where they would be staying. He led them out of the function room, into the foyer and up a flight of stairs.

The first floor was made up of one wide corridor with narrower passages branching off to the rooms. The plush carpet and golden, striped wallpaper combined to give it a regal air. They followed the man to the end of the corridor, where he showed them to adjacent rooms. They thanked him and he walked off with a slight nod of his head.

Adam's room was perfect. A double bed with a heavy wooden headboard rested against one wall; the deep red duvet and the laundered sheets looked very inviting to his weary eyes. A large television and a DVD player sat atop a sideboard opposite the bed and a radiator was fighting the chilly evening air.

This'll do nicely, he thought to himself.

He walked into the bathroom and closed the door behind him. He did his business and then washed his hands in the sink, taking in his appearance in the mirror. Gone were the straggly beard and dark circles under his eyes. Thanks to an exercise routine, a job he loved and caring about what he ate, he had never looked healthier. He unlocked the door and jumped when he entered the main bedroom again.

Damien was sitting on the edge of his bed.

'Your door was ajar so I thought I'd let myself in,' Damien explained, seeing Adam's perplexed look.

'No, it wasn't,' Adam shot back.

'Maybe I walked through the wall then, I can't quite remember. Anyway, we're going on a ghost walk. The island has many legends and it's a tradition for newcomers to hear them.'

Adam didn't care too much for ghosts.

Or Damien.

'We're not really with the party downstairs…' he started, though Damien quickly cut across him.

'Nonsense! You're a guest of the island.'

'Colin mentioned earlier that he wasn't feeling too well, so I'll have to see what he thinks.'

'Already taken care of, my friend,' Damien smiled. 'He's well up for it.'

'Great,' Adam said through gritted teeth. 'Just great.'

4

SPOOKY GOINGS ON

IF ANYONE HAPPENED to be passing by the island on a boat (impossible because of the vicious waves and roiling storm) or somehow zoomed in on it with a telescope, they'd be greeted by an odd sight.

Despite the lashing rain and rumbles of thunder; a vampire, a wrestler, a scantily-clad cat woman, an obese David Bowie and two young men wrapped up in thick coats (one of whom was having a terrible time) were huddled around a tall man dressed as a circus ringmaster.

So far, their tour guide had given them the history of their accommodation. According to him, it had been built by a wealthy family who wanted to get away from the hustle and bustle of city life in the 1700s. The construction had been plagued with difficulties and obstructions and when the house was finally finished, the family moved in, though they didn't stay for long. Historical documents, like Mr. Winkle's diary, tell of ghostly sightings and paranormal activity. When his wife awoke one morning to find her favourite pearl necklace missing, it was to be the final straw.

The family moved out and the property passed through many hands. Some stayed longer than others, but they all found a reason to leave for good in the end. In the mid-1800s, it had been used as an asylum, before passing out of use altogether when it was deemed the island was doing the lunatics more harm than good.

Finally, it had been taken over by a local entrepreneur who stripped it and made it what it was today. Sometimes, Damien said, you can still hear the screams of the unfortunate fellows who endured shock treatments and experimental medicines. Their pleas for mercy endured in the walls.

Adam hated this. He tried to act nonchalant, but tales of Winkle Island had been bandied around at school and had unsettled him then. Now that he was on the island with this ragtag bunch of presenters and the creepiest man he'd ever met, he regretted ever saying yes to the job.

They left the house behind and walked to the north of the island. The unrelenting rain felt like needles on any skin left exposed and Adam felt a pang of pity for Sophie, who must've realised by now that she had made a silly decision. At least the vampire, after some discussion about whether fancy dress rules were being broken, had given her his oversized cape to protect herself from the worst of the elements.

As they approached the cliffs, a small building swam into view. It wasn't much bigger than a garden shed and made from wooden logs, like a filming location from a Scandi Noir. Damien unhooked the snib on the front door and ushered everyone inside. They stood in what would've been a circle, had there been space. Some stamped their feet on the stained concrete floor in order to get some blood flowing to their toes; others crossed their arms over their bodies and rubbed their arms. The vampire did this, and Adam didn't know if it was to get warm or to look the part.

'This is the chapel,' Damien said, his words coming out in a mist. 'When residents of the asylum sadly passed on, they were brought here for a religious ceremony before burial. Obviously, no one from the mainland attended, hence the size of the place. Their bodies were then taken down the path to the graveyard near the house. I like to end the tour there, so you will all get to see it.'

Great, Adam thought as they were ushered out into the cold once more. *The highlight of the island is a bloody graveyard.*

As they traipsed towards the graveyard, Damien pointed out a deep well just behind a thick wall of trees. The crumbling, circular brickwork was just visible and thankfully, they weren't expected to go for a closer look. Instead, Damien picked up the pace, his enthusiasm for the burial site evident in his long strides.

After a couple of minutes, they reached a rusty gate with a dirty sign attached, announcing this as sacred ground. Beyond the gate and chain link fence, identical rectangular headstones emerged from the ground. The uneven terrain made them look like teeth inside a mouth that hadn't ever been to the dentist. Some had fallen over, though most stood tall and proud, despite being there for over a century.

Adam gazed up at the house and saw Albert and his wife in one of the windows. He was jealous that Damien had accepted their advancing years as a suitable enough excuse to avoid the tour. Damien ushered the rest of the group into the graveyard and they spent ten miserable minutes being led through the rows, listening to stories about infamous inmates of the asylum.

Adam didn't know if what Damien was telling them was true or not, but the stories chilled him anyway. Then he saw it.

A hand reaching from one of the graves. The fingernails caked with dirt and the knuckles bloodied and broken.

He let off a volley of curse words and as the presenters turned to him with confused faces, he pointed to the ground with a trembling finger. Sophie let out a yelp and Paul repeated some of Adam's choice words. Adam started to back away towards the gate, when he noticed Damien's smile.

He watched as the ringmaster bent down and pulled the prosthetic arm free of the dirt. He waved it around, much to the laughter of the group. Adam shook his head and started walking towards the warmth of the building, a perfectly cued flash of lightning lighting his way.

5

LA LUCIOLE VIOLETTE

ADAM LAY ON his bed, pleased to be feeling warm again. The shame of making a fool of himself in front of the other guests had washed away as the hot droplets from the showerhead had collided with his skin. He didn't owe them anything and, with any luck, he wouldn't have to set eyes on them for the rest of the weekend.

He opened his bag and pulled some fresh clothes out. He was happy to be free of the sodden jeans he'd been wearing before, and felt a pang of pity for the presenters who had agreed to wear the same clothes all weekend. They must be freezing after the tour.

He pulled a T-shirt, a pair of joggers and a hoodie on and stood by the radiator while he connected his laptop to the television. After a minute of fiddling, his computer screen was duplicated on the wide screen of the TV.

Let the weekend begin, he thought to himself.

He opened up a browser window and typed in the WiFi code he'd been given earlier. Once connected, he navigated to Netflix and chose an episode of Sherlock—the one where Moriarty appears for the first time.

Andrew Scott, to his mind, was the best actor to have played Sherlock's arch nemesis. Colin liked Natalie Dormer's portrayal in Elementary, but Adam reckoned that was only because he fancied her.

He threw himself onto the bed just as a brisk knock on the door sounded.

'If that's Damien,' Adam said. 'You can do one. Anyone else, come in!'

Colin poked his head around the door, a smile spreading across his face at the theme tune for his favourite show.

'Fancy an ep?' Adam asked, shuffling over to one side of the bed.

'Yeah, later. We've been invited for dinner.'

'But, we've got our weekend supplies right here.'

Adam pointed to the bag of food. Sausage rolls, Thai sweet chilli crisps and enough chocolate to rot both their teeth. Not to mention the bottles of Coke.

'I know,' Colin said. 'But, they've got a roast dinner going on downstairs. Chicken, spuds, gravy and a spread of desserts for after.'

'It'll mean mingling with those dicks, though,' said Adam.

'Worth it for a free feast.'

Adam weighed it up in his mind. He was already sold, but he needed Colin to know that he was putting up a real fight.

'Okay,' he said, standing up. 'But, if I end up next to the creepy guy, I'm leaving.'

SITTING NEXT TO the creepy guy might've been better than how it had ended up. Adam sat with Colin on one side, which was fine, but with Gavin's bulk on the other. As a six foot something, twenty-stone man, dressed in wrestling garb, it meant certain areas of his body were left exposed. Like the armpits, which were right next to Adam's face.

Worse than that, though, was that Damien was directly opposite him. Which meant intense eye contact that Adam was trying hard to avoid, but could feel boring into him.

As they waited for the food to be served, Keith stood up.

Adam had to give it to him—he had balls. He had tried hard to pull off the Bowie look. He'd squeezed himself into a sparkly silver catsuit and painted the colourful lightning bolt onto his face. However, with his straggly dark hair and considerable girth, he looked more like Rab C. Nesbitt.

He held a glass aloft. Adam thought that he had taken it upon himself to be the group's leader. Perhaps that was one of the expectations of having the prime-time slot.

'I thought it might be nice to go around the table and say what we are thankful for. It's become something of a tradition.' He glanced around at his audience. 'I'll start. This year, I am thankful for the continued opportunity to entertain the people of Stonebridge and to once more have the top-listened to show.'

He sat down and looked to his right.

'My beautiful wife,' said Albert, motioning to the lady sitting beside him.

'Getting to spend the weekend with you lot,' said Drive Time Dave.

'Love,' said Sophie.

'Love?' repeated some of the members around the table.

'Have you met someone?'

'You've kept that quiet,' said Gavin, looking put out.

'I've not told anyone because it's early days,' Sophie said. 'I don't know if it's going to go anywhere but it's feeling good.'

'So, who is the poor chap?' asked Keith.

'That, I cannot divulge. Yet,' she added, as a chorus of boos filled the room.

'Go on,' Gavin said.

'Leave the poor girl alone,' Albert said, and any more cross examination was quelled by the arrival of food. Conversation died as plates were loaded and eating commenced.

ADAM AND COLIN stood by the bar, pints in hand. It had been a long day and Adam could feel the tiredness begin to creep behind his eyes. One more pint and he'd call it a night.

The presenters were getting a bit rowdy. They'd had a few cocktails during dinner, and now that the food was gone, the drinking had begun in earnest. They sat in groups at the table, chatting and laughing while Albert fiddled with the computer at the side of the room.

A media file appeared on the fabric screen and Albert tapped a knife against the stem of his wine glass. He cleared his throat as a hush descended in the room and attention was turned to the station's owner.

'I've prepared a short video for us to watch, before I say a few words.'

He pressed play on the video and grainy black and white footage began. It showed a small building with smashed windows and missing roof tiles. A man was smiling happily at the camera, one hand on the ramshackle building as if it was his pride and joy.

Then, colour bloomed. The footage leapt on a generation. On screen was Albert, forty years ago, with thick sideburns creeping down his cheeks, wearing a flowery shirt and bell-bottom trousers. Next, some footage of Albert sitting behind a mixing desk, talking into a microphone. You couldn't hear what he was saying, but he looked like he was having a great time.

The footage continued in this vein; fond memories at Stonebridge Radio Station over the year. Laughter sounded in the room as a much younger and thinner Keith Starr walked through shot, his fingers pointing like guns at the camera.

Adam watched as present day Keith shook his head and chuckled.

The footage finished with a picture of the current stock of presenters. Albert closed the video and cleared his throat again as the presenters looked at him expectantly.

'Right, well, first of all, I want to say thank you for coming. I know we do something for Hallowe'en every year, and this feels fitting. I'm looking forward to tomorrow evening's murder mystery, and I'll expect you young ones are looking forward to a bit of a boogie after I'm done...'

Adam could see the beads of sweat forming on his forehead. It felt like he was circling what he wanted to say, as if he was building up to something.

'Unfortunately, I have some bad news. I have made the tough decision to close down the station. Revenue has been down year on year. Streaming services are taking over and there is sadly no room for local radio anymore.'

The room exploded into a storm of words. Questioning him. Cursing his decision. Cries for clemency.

Albert tried to placate them, assuring them that it was a decision forced on him by money. He was losing a lot of it, and he didn't have a lot to spare in the first place.

As the noise threatened to overwhelm again, Gavin barked at everyone to quieten. He pointed a thick finger at Albert's wife, who was sitting quietly at the end of the table. Her face was ashen.

'What about that necklace?' he said. 'Great big diamond like that's bound to be worth something. Sell it and keep the station going.'

Instinctively, Margaret's fingers flew to her jewellery. Gavin was right—it was worth a lot. The thin silver chain was valuable on its own, but the real prize was the firefly pendant. The ornate thorax of the insect was a single cut purple diamond, while the silver wings were studded with smaller purple sapphires.

Margaret held the glittering insect in a balled fist.

Albert's face reddened.

'Now, listen here. I do not owe any of you a living. That necklace is family heirloom and it's none of your business how much it's worth. I'm coming up to retirement age as it is, so you would've been out on your ears in a year's time anyway,' he said. He took a moment to compose himself and when he did speak again, his voice was softer. 'I don't want to ruin the weekend, so please, have fun and enjoy the time you have together.'

He held his hand out and his wife followed him out of the room, taking the firefly with her. The cacophony of noise started up again as Adam and Colin finished their pints.

'JESUS,' COLIN SAID as they walked up the stairs. 'A mass firing! A bit of drama for the evening.'

'And even weirder that they were all dressed in their costumes.'

'I wonder if the murder mystery will still go ahead?'

'Who cares? I plan on not leaving my room again until the boat arrives.'

They walked the length of the corridor, bade each other goodnight and entered their respective rooms. Adam's head had barely touched the pillow before he'd fallen asleep.

6

MURDER MYSTERY

COLIN AWOKE WITH a start.

It felt like he hadn't really been asleep for any considerable amount of time. The heavy thump of bass had carried through the house from the presenter's disco, though he must've drifted off, as he couldn't remember hearing the party reach an end.

The room was pitch black and the storm was roaring on outside, but aside from that, the house was quiet. He wondered what had caused him to wake. A crash of thunder? He didn't know, but a smashing sound was lingering in his thoughts. Perhaps, it was a bad dream, he thought as he rolled over.

As he pulled the duvet tightly around him, a scream sliced through the howl of the wind. He sat upright again and strained his ears. He couldn't tell whether it had come from inside or out, but surely no one would be daft enough to be outside in weather like this, especially at this time of night.

As he pushed the duvet off to go and have a peek out the window, he froze. There was another shout. A man's shout this time. It had come from down the corridor.

He reached to the bedside table and picked up his phone. It was just past three o'clock. What was going on?

He tried to ring Adam, but there was no signal, so he ran to his room instead. He knocked quietly on the door.

'Who is it?' Adam whispered from behind the heavy oak.

'Colin. Let me in.'

Adam opened the door slightly and peered out.

'You hearing this?' he said.

'Yeah, what do you think…?'

Colin's question was cut off by a noise further down the corridor. They both stopped talking to listen.

'Murder! There's been a murder!' someone screamed.

'Bloody hell,' said Adam. 'It's going to be that dickhead ringmaster doing some sort of SAS murder mystery. He's taking the piss if he thinks he can start this in the dead of night.'

Guttural cries for help sounded from behind a closed door at the end of the hallway. Colin took a few slow steps in the direction of the noise.

To his ears, the anguish in the shouts sounded too real to be those of an actor. Though, this place ran murder mysteries most weekends of the year, so those involved were probably pretty good at nailing the realism by now.

Still, this sounded too... raw.

When another shout pierced the blackness, Colin picked up the pace and arrived at the room he believed the noise was coming from. He turned the handle and burst in, half-expecting a fake crime scene, but not getting it.

This one was very real.

Albert was hovering over his wife, his hands pressed to a deep gash in her chest, trying to stem the flow of blood.

'Call an ambulance,' he yelled, and Colin took off at pace down the stairs to the reception. He figured if his mobile had no reception, then none of them would, but he'd spotted a landline behind reception when they we're checking in.

He rounded the desk and picked up the handset, dialling 999.

When it was answered, he told them the emergency and the location and was met with bad news. The storm would make it impossible for any help to arrive. It was too dangerous for boats to make the crossing and a helicopter would stand no chance of landing in the ferocious winds.

They had a short conversation about what he could do, before he hung up the phone and sprinted up the stairs again, three at a time.

He arrived to a gathering of people. A few of the presenters loitered in the doorway, swaying gently with unfocused eyes. It must've been one hell of a party.

Damien looked like he was giving a rather green looking Adam a pep talk in the corridor and, inside the room, Sophie was holding a thick towel to Margaret's wound. From the way the towel was stained a deep crimson, Colin knew it was too late.

On the floor, Albert was sitting with his back against the radiator with another towel pressed to his forearm. He looked up and saw Colin's expression, before breaking down in tears.

7

THE AFTERMATH

AN HOUR LATER, everyone had scattered.

Most had uttered their condolences and gone back to their rooms, locking the doors behind them. Adam had simply pointed to the blood-stained bed and backed out of the room.

Colin knew that a pinprick of blood was enough to send Adam woozy, so he didn't blame the guy for wanting to leave.

He did, however, think it was rather callous of the presenters not to stay and rally around their boss, supporting him in the aftermath of the murder of his wife.

But, then it dawned on him.

One of them must have been the one to have done this to him.

The island was remote and it was only the presenters, the staff and Damien here. Which meant it had to be someone in the house who had done this.

Colin made another cup of tea for the old man, who was sitting in the armchair with his eyes closed. He'd been that way for a while, and Colin hadn't wanted to disrupt him.

He had thrown a bedsheet over his wife's body so that Albert didn't have to stare at it. The vividness of the red and the ghostly white skin.

He didn't need the reminder of what had happened tonight there in front of him, though Colin was sure that the image would be stained behind Albert's eyelids for the rest of his life.

Colin set the cup of steaming tea on the circular table beside the old man, and sat on the other armchair. He angled the armchair slightly, so that when the old man opened his eyes, it would not seem like some intense interview scenario.

'How's your arm?' Colin said.

The old man responded with a shrug.

In the aftermath of what had happened, Colin had tended to the gash on Albert's arm. It was a couple of inches in length but thankfully not very deep. It would probably require a few stitches when back on the mainland, but for now, Colin had washed it as well as he could and secured it with a tight bandage.

The first aid training from his job at the Stonebridge Retirement Home had stood him in good stead.

At length, Albert opened his eyes. He glanced at Colin, then at his arm before settling on the body of his wife.

'I can't believe it,' he said, his voice hoarse and cracking. 'I just can't believe what has happened.'

His eyes never left the bed.

'Bad enough that they killed her, but they took the necklace, too. Heartless, heartless people,' he said, shaking his head. 'What did the police say?'

After attempts to stem the flow of blood had been unsuccessful and Margaret's death had been confirmed, Colin had descended the stairs once more and called the police.

They'd said the same thing as the ambulance service; the storm was too strong for any of their transport to deal with. They'd promised him that at the first sign of the storm's retreat, they'd get here. But, for now, the best that Colin could do was close the door to the room and keep the crime scene intact.

Colin had watched enough true crime shows to know that the immediate period after the crime had been committed was the most valuable. Police called it the golden hour, when material usable by the police is at its most readily available.

Judging by the weather forecast, the police were going to miss this window by a good twenty-four hours, at least.

Colin relayed the information back to the old man, who frowned and shook his head.

'They'll never catch who did this,' he said.

'Well, there's a bit of an advantage. The suspect pool is low, there can't be more than twelve people on the island. The police will ask their questions and…'

'And nothing,' Albert interrupted. 'All the evidence will have gone—whoever has done this will lie through their teeth and get away with it.'

'You sound like you don't have much faith in the police.'

He sighed.

'Over the years, the radio station has been broken into a number of times. Expensive things were stolen and I was constantly fobbed off with the "it's under investigation" line. Never heard a bloody thing back. So, no. I don't expect the police to do a damn thing about this.'

Colin knew that the police would treat a dead body differently to a set of stolen speakers, but bit his tongue. Albert didn't need to hear it. Instead, they sunk back into silence. Albert closed his eyes again.

Colin's heart went out to the man. In his job, he'd seen families attempt to deal with the death of a loved one. He'd comforted many a wife, husband, son and daughter, and seen first-hand the devastation caused by a natural death.

He couldn't imagine what this must be doing to poor Albert.

'You know,' Colin stared. 'Adam and myself have done a bit of investigating in our time.'

'I'm aware,' Albert replied. 'Your mother spoke about you when we were arranging this weekend. She's very proud of you.'

'If you like, we could ask a few questions. See if we can do anything until the police get here.'

He shrugged again.

'I just want to be left alone,' Albert said, as he began to cry.

Though it sounded like a rudely worded dismissal, Colin knew better. He'd been spoken to far worse in the past by grieving relatives.

'If you need anything, let me know,' Colin said.

He pushed himself out of the chair, opened the door and took one last look at Albert's heaving shoulders before leaving and walking to Adam's room.

IF THE SUN had risen, there would have been no way of knowing.

The already violent weather outside had seemingly stepped it up a notch, as if in retaliation against the human race's more base ideologies. Like, for example, one human life meant more than another, and so we're entitled to play God. Or, the Devil.

Rain attacked the window like mini battering rams and the dark clouds gathered and swirled, refusing to be moved on by the gale-force wind.

Adam let the curtain fall back into place, blocking out the sight of the outside world but not the sounds. He grabbed his laptop from the table and took it to the bed. He climbed in and pulled the duvet over him, prompting a shiver that had nothing to do with the cold.

He'd only ever seen one other body; that of his friend Daniel Costello who'd met his untimely end last year, though not anywhere near as violently as poor Mrs Fernsby. It was no secret Adam wasn't good with blood, though he doubted anyone on the island could bear witness to the aftermath of whatever happened in that room without the feeling that they needed to throw up.

He opened up his emails and typed the beginnings of Helena's address into the recipient box. He had no other way of getting in contact with his new girlfriend and thought that what had happened should be shared. He was midway through the body of the missive when a knock sounded on the door, before Colin made himself known.

Adam slid out of bed and unlocked the door, letting his friend in. He followed Colin to the bed and sat down on the edge.

'You okay, man?' he asked.

'Yeah. Trouble seems to follow us around.'

They both nodded, aware that empty words would do little for either of them. Something awful had happened here tonight.

Or, rather, someone had done something awful here tonight.

'I told Albert we might look into things. He told me that mum was banging on about our exploits when they met to discuss this weekend.'

Adam smiled a small smile in reply, before nodding.

'I feel bad for the old guy. And I assume we're grounded here until the storm passes. But, didn't the police say...'

'When have we ever listened to the police? They don't know their arse from their elbow in Stonebridge.'

'Fair point. Where do we start?

8

THE CRIME SCENE

ADAM HESITATED OUTSIDE the room. The heavy oak door
was the perfect barrier between him and the bloody body, but
he knew that he couldn't put it off forever. He gave Colin a nod
and watched as his friend knocked three times on the door.

'Yes?'

The voice was broken and cracked.

'Albert, it's Colin and Adam. We're here to do the thing we
discussed.'

Adam thought his wording was very clever. With the other
presenters staying in rooms on the same landing, announcing a
murder enquiry would've been unwise.

It also made Adam feel inadequate. Behind this door lay a
still body and a man shattered by grief. A long marriage quite
literally severed by a sharp blade and here were two lads who
fancied themselves as detectives, turning up to ask questions.

Before he could convince Colin that they were perhaps not
up to the task and that waiting twenty-four hours for the police
to arrive might not be a bad thing, the lock clicked and the door
swung slowly on its hinges.

Albert looked like he'd aged a hundred years in an hour. His
eyes were sunken into dark holes and a patchwork of red crossed
his face; the exertion of endless crying clear to see.

He turned wordlessly and shuffled back to his seat. Colin and
Adam entered. Colin walked to the seat he'd sat in not long ago,
while Adam closed and locked the door. Happy that the room
was secure, he crossed the floor and stood beside his friend's
chair; his back to the body on the bed.

Out of sight, out of mind, he reckoned.

Adam smiled at the old man, who accepted the silent sympathy with a nod of his head.

'Albert, we're going to ask around and see what we can find out. The necklace has to be somewhere on the island, so I'm sure it'll turn up.'

The old man nodded again.

'Albert, can you tell us what happened?'

The old man was silent for a further minute. Aside from his eyes, which glanced this way and that, the rest of his face remained still. It looked like a photograph gone wrong.

Finally, he found his voice.

'Well, after delivering the news that I'd be closing the station, myself and...' he stumbled over the word, 'myself and Margaret came up here. Too much excitement for one night. We got ourselves ready for bed and I told her to put the necklace in the safe, but she told me she was too tired and would do it in the morning.'

He asked for a glass of water and Colin rose from his seat to fetch one. He passed Albert the glass and the old man took a few loud gulps, his Adam's apple bobbing up and down, before setting it on the table beside his seat.

'We went to sleep and I woke up to a crashing sound. Like glass breaking. It was dark, and when I turned round, there was someone standing over my wife.'

'But you didn't see who?'

'No,' he said, shaking his head. 'The curtains were closed and it was very dark. I didn't have my glasses on either. No, it was more like I sensed them there, rather than seeing them. I could hear their breathing.'

'Anything you can remember about the size at all? Short, small?'

'No, sorry.'

'That's fine. What happened next?'

'Margaret screamed when she realised there was someone else in the room. I reached across, I don't know why really. Maybe to push him away, or to shield Margaret. I felt the knife go into my arm but it took a second or two for the pain to follow. I screamed when it did and fell out of bed. When I pulled myself up again, he'd stabbed Margaret and was heading for the window again.'

'You think it was a he?'

Albert shot them a confused look. Colin added to the question.

'Only you said "he'd stabbed Margaret".'

'Oh,' Albert said. 'Well, only because I assumed no woman could be capable of such an act.'

They didn't need to ask what had happened next. Colin had heard the smash of the window, and the shouting, and had run down the corridor, unable to prevent Death from snatching Margaret from Albert's grasp.

'I think that's all we need for now. Do you mind if we have a look around?'

'By all means,' Albert said, waving an open palm at the expanse of the room. 'I'm going to get a bit of fresh air.'

'You're not going out, are you? Have you seen the rain?'

'Just to the front door. I fancy a smoke.' He looked at the body, covered by the sheet. 'She was always trying to get me to give up. Said the cigarettes would be the death of me.'

He removed his raincoat from the radiator where it had just about dried after the walk from the boat. He pulled it on and winced as the fabric passed over his bandaged arm.

Watching this, Adam couldn't stop the tears coming to his eyes. Maybe the fact that he'd started going out with someone he genuinely cared about was softening him; or perhaps it was that the old man opposite him was dealing with two types of pain—the flesh and the heart.

He'd had a lucky escape and Adam's earlier concerns about tackling the case were washed away; now, he promised himself that he'd work tirelessly to get to the bottom of it.

For Albert.

For Margaret.

They watched the old man slouch out of the room, letting the door swing slowly shut behind him. It latched with a small click, and Adam and Colin got to work.

Not having gloves, they decided the best course of action was to simply have a look. It wouldn't look good when the police came and their prints were plastered all over the room like graffiti. If something caught their eye, they'd take a picture and that would be that.

They split up; as much as a pair can split up in a hotel room. What Adam meant when he suggested "splitting up" was that Colin took the side of the room with the body, and he would cover everywhere else.

He watched Colin walk towards the bed, and like The Cowardly Lion, wished he wasn't so much of a wimp sometimes.

COLIN INCHED TOWARDS the bed. Towards the unmoving mound of bedsheets.

Sometimes, he wished Adam wasn't so much of a wimp.

I mean, yeah, he got it: no one was enthralled about being in the presence of a dead body. But Adam was another case entirely.

He'd been the laughing stock at school on BCG day. The boys in his year group had been speculating on the size of the needle for weeks—someone had heard from his brother's friend's cousin that it was as thick as four normal needles.

On the day, Danny Costello had slipped an oversized joke needle to one of the nurses, who duly whipped it out after calling Adam's name. He'd vomited at the sight of it, before promptly fainting, causing a right old ruckus. The headmaster had told him to man up when he'd come to.

But, looking over at his friend now, Colin couldn't hope for a better partner. They were yin and yang and both brought different strengths.

The smell of expensive perfume wafting through the soiled sheets brought Colin back to the here and now. He knew he couldn't risk pulling back the sheets for another look at the body, so instead would bank on the images seared into his brain from the early hours.

He only needed the headline anyway. Margaret had been stabbed to death.

Instead, he cast his attention to what surrounded her. On the floor were her clothes from the night before; the bottle green dress and her low-heeled shoes. Albert had said that she was too tired to deposit the necklace in the safe, and how she discarded her expensive clothes certainly seemed to back that up.

The set of drawers beside her bed looked like they'd been here since the beginning of time. The flat top was scarred from years of objects being dragged across it and thrown on top of it.

On it now was a half-empty glass of water and a pair of glasses. Colin snapped a picture of the items, though doubted they meant anything. They'd have been there regardless of Margaret's fate.

Perhaps the water level might be lower were she still breathing, or the glasses perched atop her nose if she was having trouble sleeping and had decided to read instead.

On the floor, in the narrow gap between the drawers and the bed, lay a little silver strip of tablets, encased in miniature domes. Colin got on his hands and knees and inspected the packet as best he could. He didn't recognise the name that was printed in green over the foil packaging, but took a picture so that he could research it later.

ADAM WAS ENGROSSED in his own discoveries a few feet away.

He'd had a walk around the rest of the room, but all the action and evidence seemed to be on Margaret's side as Albert had said. Currently, he found himself on his hands and knees, staring at the carpet.

The carpet was cream, or rather, it used to be. Decades of different footsteps; some heavy and some light, had flattened and stained the once extravagantly thick shag. The flattened areas told their own stories; plotted journeys from bed to en-suite bathroom and back again.

But these lost footprints were not what was of interest to Adam. No, he was more concerned with the residual dirt left behind from a recent visitor. Not enough muck to leave a traceable footprint, but evidence enough that someone had climbed through the window with murder on their mind.

Or, if not murder, definitely money.

Adam had watched enough true crime shows to know that death was sometimes a secondary notion. Gain was usually the first—and in this case, the gain was the necklace. The money it would bring when it could be flogged on the mainland.

Adam followed the mucky tracks from the window to the bed (as close as he dared to the body) and back again. There wasn't anything more he could tell—no outline, no size nor tread that they could match should they request everyone hand in their shoes for examination.

He stood up when he got to the window and took in the ragged, shattered glass in the lower left-hand corner of the pane. Rain smashed against the glass and the wind poured through the hole, there in the room like an unknown presence were it not for the shrill whistle it brought along with it.

Looking down, Adam could see a trellis attached to the exterior wall. It was hard to make out any detail, such was the angle. This would require a trip outside, which, given the weather, was not an exciting prospect.

'Got what we need?' asked Colin, breaking their collective silence.

'Almost,' replied Adam, pointing outside.

They both groaned.

9

LOOKING IN

THEY LEFT ALBERT'S room and walked back up the corridor to their own rooms to collect their coats.

'You know,' Colin said as they reached their doors, 'it's kind of a one-man job, isn't it?'

'Is it?' Adam asked.

'Well, all one of us has to do is go and have a look at the trellis.'

'One of us...'

'Well, yeah.'

'And which one of us would that be?'

'Allow me to put my case forward for it being you. I was the first on scene at the murder. I helped with the first aid on Albert and I was the one who did the dirty work near the body, while you looked at some muck on the floor.'

Colin cocked an eyebrow at Adam, challenging him; though his friend couldn't muster much of a counter-argument. Instead, Adam nodded his head solemnly and reached for his door handle.

'Seriously, though,' Colin said. 'We've been up half the night, so it might be wise for each of us to have a rest. I'll get some sleep now while you do this, and in a while, we'll talk about our next move.'

'Sounds like a plan,' Adam said.

Colin disappeared into his room with a swift goodbye. Adam opened his own door and entered the room. He made use of the bathroom and then grabbed his still-wet coat from the hook by the door. He looked out his window, at the darkness that lay beyond, sighed, and closed the door again.

He walked down the hall, his eyes poring over the doors that lined the corridor as he went.

He thought about what awaited the occupants upon awakening, if they were asleep at all. Tragedy loomed; some, like sober Sophie, would awake knowing that she had played a small part in trying to save a life. She might feel like a hero, knowing she'd at least done something. Or, she might feel the total opposite; a failure who had been unable to prevent a soul from drifting away into the ether.

The other presenters might awake to the news like it's the first they've heard of it, despite all four of them standing in the doorway. Some might remember nothing at all, thanks to the amount of alcohol consumed. Some might rouse, snatching at a half-remembered dream until the reality came rushing in at the sight of Albert.

His injured arm.

His dead wife.

One person would wake with an expensive necklace secreted somewhere in their room, checking their hiding place nervously as they waited for the storm to abate.

Adam walked slowly down the stairs and across the foyer to the porch. Inside the porch, to the left of the door, was a shoe rack. On it, and next to it, were several pairs of shoes and the green wellies kept by the hotel for those travellers who had come ill-prepared for a walking tour.

Currently, there was a pair of wellies for each of the party who had been for the walk last night, save for Damien who had brought his own, and Gavin who was wearing a pair of huge Doc Martens as part of his wrestling get-up.

Adam found the pair he had discarded last night upon arriving back from the ghost walk, and winced as the wet soles immediately soaked his socks.

He pulled open the door and peeked outside. There was no sign of Albert. He must've finished his cigarette and gone back to his room, or, more likely, thought better of going outside when faced with the cold and rain.

Adam pulled the hood over his head, pulled the drawstrings so tight that he resembled Kenny from South Park, and stepped into the storm.

WITHIN SECONDS OF closing the door behind him, his cheeks were numb and his nose was bright red, though not luminous enough to make a dent in the darkness that surrounded him.

The wind felt like it was zeroing in on him and him alone; the gusts catching his hood like a parachute and forcing him backwards. He reckoned if anyone was looking out a window at him now, it wouldn't look too dissimilar to the video for Michael Jackson's Earth Song.

He fished his phone from his pocket and turned the torch on. He held it out in front of him, trying to protect the screen from the downpour as much as he could, and set off. He tried to hug the building as closely as possible, though it afforded little protection.

He edged past windows, slipping occasionally in the flowerbeds and grass which had more of the consistency of quicksand to it. Thankfully, childhood had always placed quite an importance on how to evade such granular matter, so it didn't hold him up for too long.

Finally, he arrived under Albert's window. Luckily, the light was still on and the curtains open, as they had been when he and Colin had left. This meant he could put his phone away and use the light from the room. It made him feel like he was on some divine quest, bathed in ethereal light from above.

Though, there was nothing divine about what he was doing, slinking about in the darkness and the mud, looking for clues that could lead to them finding a killer. If anything, it was a quest sent from Beelzebub.

He reached out and pulled at the trellis. It was made from a heavy wood and painted white, though a long time ago. The original oak colouring was shining through where the white had started to peel. Ivy crept up the wooden structure, spreading in a triangular shape as it stretched past the window and reached for the roof. The leaves dropped water on Adam's exposed hand like a waterfall, and he uttered a few curse words under his breath as his skin turned to ice.

The trellis was attached securely to the wall, barely moving at all when Adam shook it. He figured that it could easily support someone who wanted to climb it.

Adam was half-temped to try and climb it himself, but the wooden trellis and the ivy were slick with water and, if he fell, there was no telling how much damage he'd do to himself. And anyway, the door to Albert's bedroom had been locked from the inside and all the evidence pointed to the killer entering via the window above Adam's head.

Sherlock Holmes wouldn't need to climb the trellis to reach that conclusion, so neither did he.

Instead, he cast his eyes to the ground. The area underneath Albert's window was partially protected from the rain by an overhanging triangular section of roof. It hadn't done a lot to keep the ground dry, it was only slightly less marshy than the rest of the island, but it had helped with one thing.

In amongst the drowning flowers, was a footprint. It was facing towards the wall and looked like the print of a welly boot. The heel area had a firm imprint on the soil, though the toe area was not as defined.

Adam tried putting his foot beside it to gauge what size it might be in comparison to his size nine, though it was impossible to tell due to the front section that faded without an end. Glass crunched under the sole of his shoe, and for a second he was worried he'd impaled himself.

Still, at least he could tell conclusively that someone had come through the flowerbed, ascended the trellis, broken the window and killed, before making their escape the same way.

Adam got out his phone again and opened the camera app. He pressed the button to take a photo, and as the flash blossomed, something in the treeline opposite moved.

Adam killed the phone light and flattened himself hard against the wall, trying with all his might to sink through the brickwork like some sort of character from The X-Files.

He peered into the darkness, searching for any flicker of evidence that whatever had moved was coming his way. After a few minutes, when he had convinced himself that he had imagined it, or that it was simply an animal he had startled with his burst of light, he started to breathe audibly again.

Damien's stories swirled around his head. Branches and wind morphed into ghouls and banshee's wails. Adam counted to three in his head and ran as fast as he could to the front door, only pausing for breath once he was safely entrenched in the entrance hall.

His eyes briefly lingered on the wellies again, realising that he was no safer in here than out there. Though, in here, the monsters were real.

He set off again at full pace, up the stairs and down the corridor. He fumbled for his keys with his frozen hands, shoving them in the keyhole at the third time of asking.

He locked the door behind him and slid down the back of it.

Finally, he allowed himself a laugh.

What had they got themselves involved in this time?

10

THE BROTHERS OF DESTRUCTION AND
THE MINISTRY OF DARKNESS

OUTSIDE, THE CLOUDS formed a black patchwork; its seams so tightly knitted they could not be seen. They rolled this way and that across the sky, an embargo mission against the sun's rays.

And they were bang up to the task.

Inside room number nine, whatever was happening outside was of no importance to Adam. If he could've, he'd gladly have locked his door from the inside and swallowed the key. He'd happily have waited for the police to kick down his door or, less fun, use a spare key from reception to free him from his haven; the killer having been apprehended and already on his way back to Stonebridge.

But that wasn't going to happen anytime soon.

It had taken quite a while for his heart to resume a normal rhythm inside his chest. He'd liked to have taken Colin's advice and get some shut-eye, but the slightest noise or rustle of curtain in the draught took him back outside, when he had pressed himself against the wall and waited for the killer to emerge from the treeline.

Instead of hiding under the duvet waiting for Johnny Nod, he was at his computer. He finished his email to Helena, providing her with a detailed account of his sleepless night, though he had hovered over the send button for long enough to know that sending it was a bad idea.

Without phone signal, it was cruel. To tell her he was essentially locked in a building with a thief and a killer who was unafraid to stab an elderly couple was a bad idea. To tell her that he was actively trying to find said rogue was even worse.

In the end, he'd deleted the email and had instead been using his time to gather as much background information on his potential quarry as possible.

Stonebridge wasn't exactly the centre of the universe and the presenters were definitely not household names. Information was taken from the Stonebridge Gazette's archives, the Stonebridge Radio Station's website or from their own social media accounts.

He scribbled down as much as he could, compiling a fact file on each. It wasn't much to go on, but something was better than nothing.

He'd then turned his attention to Damien, but without even knowing if it was his real name, he didn't get very far. There were a few photos of him on the website for this hotel; staring at the camera solemnly from the edge of group pictures, as if that week's party had asked him to be part of their memory and he couldn't think of anything worse, but couldn't decline either.

Adam closed the lid of his laptop, got up and walked across the room to the door. He summoned the courage to unlock it, took a deep breath and eased it open a few inches.

There was no one there.

He pulled it back further to reveal an empty corridor.

He slinked out of his own room and knocked on Colin's door. He waited a few minutes and knocked again, this time hearing his friend's annoyed mutterings.

A minute later, the door opened slowly to reveal a bleary-eyed Colin, his hair pointing in all directions like a malfunctioning compass. He checked his watch, though all it told him was that he hadn't had the amount of sleep he had wanted, before fixing his eyes on Adam.

'You've got a date with the wrestler,' Adam said, handing him the page containing the information he'd managed to find on one Gavin Callaway.

'Thanks,' Colin croaked.

'I'd say put some clothes on, but wrestlers tend to do their best work in not much more than boxers. It might be the way in to Gavin's world.'

Adam backed away before Colin could connect with the punch that was aimed at his arm.

FULLY DRESSED AND with a coffee down him, Colin was feeling more alive. Well, as alive as three hours sleep and a hit of caffeine can make you.

He dragged the spoon through the second milky coffee and set it on the table. He picked up the piece of paper Adam had given him and read over the notable and newsworthy parts of Gavin's life.

Which amounted to one main point; but quite a telling one.

He leaned back in his chair and supped at his drink, trying to prepare himself for his chat with Gavin. He didn't know how to broach the subject on the paper, and wasn't sure he wanted to in a room with just the two of them in it.

He puffed out his cheeks, stood up and walked towards the door. At least Adam knew that he was meeting the man dressed as the wrestler. If something were to happen to Colin, at least they'd have an answer to the question that they were poking at.

HAVING KNOCKED ON the door a number of times, Colin came to three conclusions.

One. That, behind the door, Gavin might be dead. Dispatched in the same way as poor Margaret Fernsby.

Two. That, behind the door, Gavin might be passed out drunk. Colin had heard the pulse of loud music long into the early hours of the morning and had seen Gavin swaying in Albert's doorway as Margaret's life had ebbed away. Such a sight might drive an already drunk man to more drink.

Three. That, behind the door, there was no Gavin. That he was simply somewhere else; safe, sound and doing all he could to drive the lingering remnants of alcohol from his bloodstream.

Colin thumped the door one last time and set off to find the missing man. The relentless thrum of rain on the roof told Colin that Gavin would more than likely be somewhere within the confines of the hotel.

Unless he was some sort of Bear Grylls type.

Which, it turns out, he wasn't.

Whereas the intrepid television explorer liked to drink his own urine from a recently hollowed out snake corpse, Gavin was much more of your deal-with-your-problems-with-a-stiff-drink type of guy.

Colin found him slumped against the bar, a hand curled around a small tumbler, and a bottle of whiskey his only company.

Colin cleared his throat to announce his arrival.

Though it was fairly dark in the room, Gavin took his chin off his hand and squinted at Colin with almost closed eyes.

Less about the amount of light and more about the numbers of me he's seeing, thought Colin.

Colin introduced himself and got a loud grunt in reply. Though, it seemed, the grunt was merely a precursor to Gavin pushing himself off the bar and hefting his enormous frame to its full height.

Gavin was truly something. On a normal day, he'd be tall. Today, with his platform boots on, he was pushing seven foot. His spandex vest and sheer tights showed a body once toned and cared for, but now let off the leash a bit. Long strands of hair from a black wig fell onto his wide shoulders. His get up fell somewhere between funny and threatening.

He held out a bear-like paw which he used to squash Colin's fingers into one single digit.

Still without words, he sat down on the bar stool he was calling home and held the glass aloft, wordlessly asking if Colin wanted to join him in a dram. Seeing an opportunity for getting his foot in the door, Colin nodded. Gavin reached over the bar and procured a clean glass, which he slid along the wooden bar top and into Colin's waiting hand.

Within a minute, he'd filled Colin's glass and refilled his own and was looking at Colin with bleary eyes.

'Who are you again?'

'Colin McLaughlin,' he replied. 'I was here to set up the screen and the computer and stuff for tonight's murder mystery.'

'Looks like you wasted a trip, brother. We got the real thing last night.'

He took a slug from his glass as if the mention of last night's events needed to be washed away.

'Dreadful, isn't it?'

'Just awful,' Gavin replied. 'You know, Margaret and Albert were very good to me a few years back. Gave me a chance when not many would've done.'

Colin already knew the story, thanks to Adam's research, but hearing it first hand, unprompted, would be even better.

'How do you mean?'

Gavin drained the glass before beginning his story.

'Well, as everyone knows everything about everyone in Stonebridge, I don't imagine I'm telling you anything new. But, I used to work in the city, doing pretty well for myself. I was in a club one night, and this weedy wee fella was cracking onto a girl and I could see that she was uncomfortable.'

'You got involved?'

'Aye. My sister would've been about that age and I had this vision of this creep doing the same thing to her. So, I told him to leave it. Polite, at first, but he gave a bit of mouth back. I asked him again, less polite this time, to back off. He swung for me, but I saw it coming a mile away. I moved out of the way and... retaliated.'

He didn't relay any more information, and didn't need to. Colin had seen the photo of the boy. He looked the cocky type, even with two black eyes and a couple of missing teeth.

'Anyway, I was sentenced to some jail time. Lost my job and my girl.'

He looked mournfully at the ceiling, as if trying to summon some retrospective divine intervention.

When none came, he pressed on.

'It was hell and, let me tell you, I paid for my mistakes in there. When I was released a few years back, I came back to

Stonebridge. I was treated like a leper by my old "friends" and at one stage, I considered... you know...'

He pulled a finger swiftly across his throat.

'That's a dreadful thing to say, isn't it? Considering what has happened to poor Margaret, considering it was her and Albert that saved me.'

'How?' Colin asked.

'We got talking one day. Chance meeting in a coffee shop. I recognised him as the owner of the station, and I told him about how I got into radio presenting in prison. They try to teach you new skills and I was always into my music. Those weekly sessions really got me through. So, next thing I know, he's telling me that one of his presenters is having a baby and inviting me down to try out.'

'And it went well?'

'It went okay. I think he felt sorry for me, more than anything. There aren't many listeners on the 4am-7am show, so I think he thought I couldn't do too much wrong.'

Now that he'd got him loosened up and talking, Colin switched tack.

'You seemed quite angry last night.'

Gavin fixed Colin with a stare that would cause a statue to have bowel movements. Colin looked away as Gavin began to speak.

'Put yourself in my shoes, kid. Ex-con doing the graveyard shift on local radio. It's hardly the morning show on Radio One, is it? I'm not really raking it in, so when he told me he was essentially firing me, yeah, you could say I was angry. But, I had nothing to do with what happened, if that's what you're implying.'

'You pointed out the necklace.'

'You know what...' he said, raising himself up from his stool. 'I don't like what you're getting at here. Yeah, I pointed out the necklace. It doesn't take Mr Cartier to know that the necklace with huge purple diamonds might be worth a quid or two. Sell that, save the business is all I was pointing out.'

Colin couldn't help but notice the flecks of spittle that had taken residence in Gavin's thick beard. Or, the manic look in his eyes.

'Do you think one of the other presenters might have had something to do with what happened to Margaret?'

Now that he was out of the scope's sights, Gavin seemed to relax slightly. He once again fell onto his seat and topped up his glass. He swirled the contents, and the look may have had more gravitas if the amber liquid wasn't spilling with each flick of the wrist.

'You know, I barely know them. I know they are generally self-serving, ambitious people who would throw you overboard if it meant a shot at having a better show... Having the middle of the night slot has rendered me an unworthy friend.'

He took a sip, and stared at the glass, as if to question where the rest of the whiskey had gone.

'Do I think one of them could've killed Margaret and taken the necklace? Absolutely I do.'

He finished his glass, thumped it against the bar and got to his feet once more. He leaned in close to Colin, who got an uninhibited blast of the sweat and alcohol emptying from Gavin's pores.

'It might be worth having a word with Dave,' he said, before burping loudly. He wafted away the smell without apology. 'He was absent for quite a while from the party, and rumours have it that he could do with a bit of extra cash at the minute.'

He touched his nose conspiratorially, before marching off across the would-be dancefloor and out of the room.

Colin pushed his untouched glass away. He'd heard it said once that there was a special rung in Hell reserved for those who wasted good whiskey, but currently, he had his own devils to dance with.

He followed Gavin out of the room.

11

BAD BLOOD

DRACULA OPENED THE door and gave Adam a look.

Not an "I want to suck your blood" look. More a "who the hell are you and why are you knocking on my door" type.

But then, nothing about Drive Time Dave looked very much like a vampire. What was left of his dark hair was racing back from his forehead and a small mouth held captive oversized front teeth like some sort of prisoner of war camp; the conditions not quite up to scratch. He was about the same height as Adam, though slightly hunched, like sitting behind a mic all these years had wreaked havoc with his posture.

Instead of welcoming Adam in, or telling him where to get to, he simply left the door open and walked back to the bed. He picked up his mobile and held it to his ear.

Unsure of what to do, Adam hovered at the entrance for a minute or so, before coming to the conclusion that an open door was not a closed one, so walked into the room and shut the door behind him.

He stood leaning against the mahogany desk, watching Dave. A stream of consciousness rumbled from the phone, and Adam could only pick out a word or two here and there, before realising that it was commentary of a horse race.

'Is it not on TV?' Adam asked, only getting a wide-eyed glare for an answer.

Suddenly, the commentator got very excited, his words tumbling out now, causing Dave to assume a jockey like pose on the bed. He rocked his hips in time with the rhythm of the words and Adam started to feel uncomfortable at the strange show of obscenity.

'Arigato Shuko Sho!' the vampire suddenly thundered, jumping off the bed and holding Adam in a celebratory hug. He released Adam and crossed the room, pulled the mini bar's door open and retrieved himself a can of ice-cold beer.

'Celebrating?'

'Too right I am. Big win!'

'Isn't a bit early for horse racing to be kicking off?' Adam asked.

'Maybe here, but not in the land of the rising sun.'

'Japan?'

'Someone got their geography O-level,' Dave laughed, as he crossed the room again and settled on the bed. Adam reflected on the information he had acquired from the internet. This live demonstration of brokenness was a big fat tick of validity.

Drive Time Dave had a gambling problem.

He also had a drinking problem, too, if him necking a can of lager at this time of the morning was anything to go by.

Still, one problem at a time.

'Albert just wanted us to check if everyone was okay, after last night, you know?' Adam started. 'Obviously, he's in no fit state.'

'Yeah, totally. That was some messed up shiz.'

'He also asked us to do a little bit of digging into what happened. Did you know the firefly necklace is gone?'

'You're kidding? Oh, no. I mean, losing your wife is bad enough, but losing valuable jewellery… that's going overboard.'

'Valuable? How do you know?'

'Well… I assumed,' Dave said. 'They were fairly well to do and a big purple stone like that I assume cost a pretty penny.'

'It has to be somewhere on the island. Do you think any of your fellow employees could have taken it?'

Dave seemed to study the ingredients of his lager for a moment too long. When he looked up, there was fire in his eyes.

'Employees is a funny word, considering we've all just been let go.'

'You know what I mean.'

'Yeah, I do know. Anyone of that lot is capable of anything. Gavin is an untrustworthy jailbird, Keith is the star of the station and would not have taken kindly to being tossed to the kerb like the rest of us. And Sophie? She might be the worst of all.'

'Why?'

'She's a woman. And women are the devil.'

Quite a forthright view, Adam thought. He wondered if he could needle that point any further.

'What did she do?'

'Oh, you know, came in to the station with flesh showing, laughing at everything Albert said. Suddenly, she's got the afternoon show. I've been there for ten years, paying my dues, and she shoots up the ladder right past me.'

He held up a finger to Adam and scrolled through his phone, hurriedly pressing buttons. He shot up from the bed, grabbed his jacket from the back of the chair and made for the door.

'Everything okay?' Adam asked.

'Just lumping a few quid on Hotaru in the six fifteen. Japanese standard time that is, not GMT. Smoke,' he said, holding up a packet of cigarettes. 'I get nervous before a race and these calm me down a bit. You want one?'

Adam nodded. He wasn't a smoker; in fact, he hated cigarettes, but felt he was getting somewhere and didn't want to plug the reservoir as it was emptying.

Dressed in his vampire costume, Dave looked at home in the unlit wide corridors, as if he was made to lurk in shadows; the dimness of a radio studio, the dark corners of gambling debt. It was where he felt comfortable.

They descended the stairs and walked to the door. Dave pulled a cigarette from his pocket, unbent it and shoved it between his lips. He lit it with a disposable lighter and then opened the door.

Figuring he'd got the headline about the other presenters (the headline being no one could be trusted in the eyes of Drive Time Dave), Adam decided to change lane.

'You often bet on international horse racing?'

'Yeah, sometimes virtual horse racing if there are no real races on.'

'As in, computer generated horses? But, surely that's just luck. There can't be odds or anything.'

'It's all luck, friend,' Dave said, with a grimace. 'You soon realise that. The numbers stop meaning anything and you go with your gut.'

'And how's your gut?'

Dave considered the question for a while, his cigarette disappearing in a haze of ash and smoke. With a quarter of it left, he threw it on the ground outside the door, the weather doing a foot's job of extinguishing it fully. He pulled the door closed again and rubbed his arms, the international signal for "I'm a bit cold".

'My gut has not been great these past years. It's no secret that I'm in a lot of debt. My wife left, or rather, she kicked me out. She stayed in the house and I live in a crappy little flat on the outskirts of town. Jesus,' he laughed. 'I can't even afford a place in the centre of Stonebridge! That should show you just how bad things are.'

'So, I imagine the news of your unemployment made you pretty mad?'

'Don't think I can't see what you're doing,' he said, pulling another cigarette from his pocket and shoving it behind his ear. 'If you think I had something to do with this, you're barking up the wrong tree.'

'We're just trying to eliminate people. To help Albert. Someone said they saw you leave the party…'

'Screw Albert and screw whoever told you that,' the vampire spat. 'Yeah, I left the party. I didn't feel like dancing. If that's an offence, fire me. Oh, wait. You can't. I don't have a job.'

He's rattled, Adam thought. Time to go for broke.

'So, the necklace might come in handy?'

Without warning, the vampire launched at Adam, pinning him the wall with a forearm across the neck. Adam pulled at his restraint but to no avail. For a split second, Adam had the ridiculous notion that his neck was about to be pierced by two long fangs. Though, taking in the fury burning in Dave's eyes, maybe the idea wasn't so ridiculous after all.

'How many different languages do I have to say this in. I did not take the sodding necklace.'

They stared at each other for what seemed like an eternity, before Dave released his grip and walked away.

'Sorry, man,' Adam called after him, once he was sure his voice box was working. 'We're just trying to help.'

He watched the vampire skulk off to the stairs, where he was swallowed once more by the darkness.

Adam stayed in the entranceway for a while, rubbing his neck and thinking about Dave. He had a temper, that was for sure. And a very valid reason for stealing the necklace.

When he was sure that he'd left enough time for Nosferatu to return to his lair, Adam got to his feet and made for Colin's room for a catch up, taking the stairs three at a time.

12

BENEATH THE SHEETS

ADAM PULLED HIS coffee closer and let the warmth of it filter through his hands. He pulled a white sachet from the little tub of condiments on the table and tore the top off. Normally, one sugar would suffice, but today was not a normal day.

He stirred the granules into his drink, the tinkling of spoon on china the only sound to be heard in the hotel's cafeteria, save for footsteps of his returning friend.

'Better?' Adam asked.

'Are you asking me how my toilet experience was? Having a girlfriend really has changed you.'

Adam threw the empty sugar packet at his friend, but missed. He adopted a hushed voice.

'So, what did you find out?'

Before answering, Colin took a sip of his tea.

'Well, Gavin is a huge ex-con with an eye for jewellery it would seem, though he claimed it wouldn't take a dummy to realise that the firefly necklace was worth a penny or two. He may also be a functioning alcoholic.'

'Do you think he could've killed Margaret?'

'I wouldn't rule him out. Obviously, I'd like to believe in the justice system and the power of rehabilitation, but he is a bit scary. What about Dave?'

Adam relayed what he had learned about Drive Time Dave; drowning in debt, addicted to gambling, pissed off that he's been fired and more than capable of physical assault. Adam pulled down the neck of his T-shirt to show his friend the beginnings of a bruise.

'Quite the unlikeable bunch!' Colin laughed.

'I could've told you that before spending a weekend with them.'

'What's next?'

'We talk to the others—Sophie and Keith. Damien, too. I know he's not in their crew, but he's a creepy so and so.' Adam shivered at the memory of the circus ringmaster reclining on his bed.

'It might be worth having another word with Albert too,' Colin said. 'Maybe now that he's had a while to think about it, some new memory might have been shaken loose.'

'Who should we start with?'

'Sophie, I think. You mentioned that Dave reckons she is the most capable of all of them.'

'Aye,' Adam snorted, 'but that's only because she's a woman. His views would've been outdated in the fifties.'

'Well, we'll see what we can find out from her and Keith, and then we can go back to Albert with some findings.'

'Sorted, then,' said Adam. 'Now, where are the toilets?'

Colin gave directions and Adam followed them—out the main door, down the corridor, to the right and to the left. His steps led him the back of the building where he hadn't ventured before. The furnishing was in keeping with the rest of the place, wooden panelled walls and framed pictures of old dudes and places.

The toilets were much the same. Adam did his business, aware that he was feeling watched by a painting above the urinals with eyes that moved where you did. He half-expected some sort of Scooby-Doo stuff to happen—the painted eyes sliding away to reveal human peepers or something like that.

But it didn't, thankfully.

He washed his hands and made his way back into the corridor. He turned left and walked to the end of the hallway, realising with a start that he had turned the wrong way out of the toilet and was off reservation. As he began to turn, something caught his attention.

He was now at the back of the hotel. Outside the window, he could make out a small decking area with a number of chairs and tables on it. He figured they must be bolted down, as the gale force winds would surely have made playthings of them had they not been.

Beyond the decking was a wall of black cloud, though on a clear day, the view would probably be stunning.

All of these thoughts came later, however, as the thing that had snagged his attention was front and centre in his brain.

Lying in the small conservatory that led to the outside area was a mound of blankets.

He didn't have to look any closer to know that it was another body.

And he didn't look any closer.

In fact, within the blink of an eye, he was halfway down the corridor, aiming to put as much ground between him and the body as possible.

COLIN TOOK IN Adam's sweaty, pale face, the speed with which he crossed the room and his voice three octaves higher than it usually was.

'The toilets aren't that bad,' Colin said, with a smile, which Adam did not return.

Instead, he picked up a napkin and dabbed his forehead and top lip, wiping the sweat away.

He glanced around the room, like there might be something spooky hiding in the corner, before leaning across the table and whispering in Colin's ear.

'You what?' Colin whispered back.

Adam repeated his information.

'Albert's been murdered?' Colin repeated. He looked at his friend with doubt in his eyes.

Adam quickly told his friend what he had seen, though Colin still looked doubtful. The colour rose in Adam's cheeks and he pushed back his chair.

'I know what I've seen,' Adam muttered. 'Let's go find out.'

'I THOUGHT YOU said it was at the back of the hotel.'

They were walking up the stairs, away from the area where the body supposedly lay.

'Yeah, it bloody is, but I don't want to be the one to pull back the sheet and look into those glassy eyes, do you?' Adam asked.

'Fair point. So, what's the plan?'

'We knock on Albert's door. He's not going to answer. That's our proof.'

Colin looked doubtful.

'He might be asleep, or, he might be out and about.'

'Out and about? Where would he go? Down the high street? Cinema? We're on a bloody island, it's chucking it down and his wife has just died.'

'We'll see.'

They reached the top of the stairs and marched up the corridor. Adam hammered on the door.

Silence.

'See?' he mouthed at Colin.

Colin knocked again.

'Give me a minute,' came a voice from behind the door.

The sureness fell from Adam's face as the lock turned and the door opened. There stood Albert in all his faded glory.

'Everything okay, boys?' he asked.

'You're okay?'

'Well, my wife was killed not long ago, so not quite okay.'

While Colin engaged in small talk, Adam's mind drifted. If Albert was alive and well (or, if not quite *well*, alive at least), who was buried below the sheets?

'You did what?' Colin asked, bringing Adam out of his revery.

'Well, Keith suggested it. He said that it would be better if she was out of the room, because then at least I could get some rest. I thought it was a bad idea, like you said, the police wanted the body left where it was, but he told me that we would put her somewhere safe and respectful and that the authorities would understand.'

'So, you put her in the conservatory?'

Albert suddenly looked like a little boy who was being told off by his father for participating in a half-thought-out, hair-brained scheme. Adam felt a pang of pity, which didn't last for long, as the door was slammed in their faces.

13

CAT'S GOT CLAWS

ADAM AND COLIN were holed up in the latter's bedroom, one at the foot of the bed and the other in the hard-backed desk chair.

'Do you think Keith was really looking out for Albert's best interests or…' Adam started.

'Or did he suggest moving the body so that evidence is lost? We won't know until we talk to him, but the police are going to be pissed either way.'

'Surely a man with that gut has watched enough cop shows to know that the police want to see the body where the bad thing happened.'

Adam rolled the next steps around his head.

'So, we need to talk to Keith next?'

Colin shook his head.

'I think we stick to the plan. If we go straight to Keith, it'll tip him off that we know something and who knows what he'll do. I'll go talk to Sophie and see what she says, and then you can go talk to Keith afterwards.'

'Why do we need to speak to him at all?'

'Because, if we don't and he hears we've been talking to everyone else, he'll know were onto him. We'll simply be crossing our Ts and dotting our lower case Js, and then when the police arrive after this bloody storm dies down, we can tell them everything we know.'

Adam considered this, and found only one slight chink in the armour.

'So, let me get this straight. You get to go chat to the fit blonde, and I get to speak with the overweight murderer?'

'Apparent murderer. We don't know for certain yet. And, think of it as a favour that I'm doing you. Helena wouldn't like it if she heard rumours of you and another lady having a quiet chat in a locked room.'

'And how would those rumours possibly get out?'

Colin shrugged his shoulders, but the die was cast.

'Well,' Adam huffed. 'Off you go then. I'm going to try and get some more rest.'

'In my bed?' Colin asked. 'I'm aware of your level of hygiene. Go to your own.'

Adam gave him the middle finger in reply.

SOPHIE SAUNDERS OPENED the door with an air of inevitability. Her blonde hair was pulled back into a tight ponytail and an oversized black turtleneck jumper was tasked with keeping her warm.

Having spoken to half the presenters already, it was unlikely their investigation was going to remain under wraps for long.

'YOU HERE TO interrogate me?' she said.

The question sounded cold, despite the warm smile she had plastered on her face.

'I was wondering if you wouldn't mind answering a few questions,' he nodded.

'Sure, but not here.'

She grabbed a heavy raincoat from the back of her door and joined Colin in the corridor. Wordlessly, they walked down the stairs—Colin half a step behind—to the front door. The weather was still unforgiving, though Sophie didn't seem to mind. She stepped outside, accepted the storm's embrace, and marched up the path.

Colin swore under his breath and followed her, picking up his pace so that he could catch up with her.

'Where are we going?' he shouted, though the wind stole his words as they left his lips.

They retraced their steps from the night before. Before the heartache and the knife and the broken body. They walked past the graveyard, past the trees and eventually came to the small chapel. Sophie unhooked the snib and they went in.

The chapel at least offered shelter, if not warmth. Colin took off his jacket and threw it over the back of one of the two chairs in the room. The pitter-patter of dripping water seemed to echo in the confined space. Sophie kept hers on and slipped into the chair opposite.

'Why here?' Colin asked.

'It's the only place on the island with a roof aside from the hotel, and I can't be there at the minute. I keep thinking about the body. Her eyes. Staring...'

She puffed out her cheeks and closed her eyes, as if the images had followed the pair on the breeze and invaded the holy space.

'So, you're trying to get to the bottom of what happened then?'

Colin nodded.

'You know,' she went on, 'I've heard of the two of you. You're like the north coast's unofficial detective team. Where's the other one?'

'Sleeping,' he replied. 'It was quite a long night.'

'I'm glad it's you. I was hoping I'd get the handsome one.'

She cocked an eyebrow and Colin felt his face burn red.

'So, what do you want to know?' she asked.

'Do you know Albert and Margaret well?' he asked, knowing that it was a poor opener. He needed to regain his composure, ease himself in.

'Well, obviously Albert was my boss, so I knew him well. Margaret, not so much. She never really came to the station.'

'Was Albert a good boss?'

'He was a great boss,' she replied. 'He was passionate about the music, about the station and about making sure everyone was happy. Which we all were until last night.'

'Yeah, sorry about that,' Colin said. 'Can't be easy to find out you're getting fired like that.'

'Especially...' she started, though trailed off with a shake of her head.

Instead of jumping in, Colin waited, letting the silence expand between them. Someone had to fill it, and his money was on the one who talked for a living. If he was a betting man, he would've been celebrating ten seconds later.

'Especially,' she repeated, 'because he had just promoted me to the prime-time slot. I was due to start in the new year.'

'Is Keith leaving?'

'Nope, he was going to take my afternoon show.'

'Did he know?'

'I'm not sure Albert told him, but I did last night,' she shrugged. 'Albert told me in confidence, but now that the station is closing, it doesn't matter, does it?'

Colin tried to think about the wording of his next question carefully.

'Why you?'

'Why me what?' she said.

'Why did you get picked for the prime-time show? Dave and Gavin have both been there for longer, and Keith is nowhere near retirement age.'

'You think because I'm a woman I had to cast some sort of spell over poor old Albert? That there had to be some sort of deficiency in everyone else? How about the fact that I'm simply more talented than all those other losers?'

'That's a good enough reason for me.'

'You think I don't know what the others say about me? That I must be offering Albert "something" in return for the promotions. Gavin was in jail, Dave is up to his eyeballs in debt, and Keith is well past his sell by date. Seriously, the dude has never played a single record from this century! To be honest, I'm surprised it's taken this long for Albert to offer it to me.'

'You're angry with Albert?'

'Yes,' she nodded. 'I know it's only local radio, but prime-time still means something. It showed that my talents were being recognised. You should've heard Keith last night when I told him that he was going to be demoted. He was fuming!'

She laughed then. A shrill laugh with no humour in it. The wind buffeted their cliffside haven, causing the ancient windows to rattle in their frames. Sophie looked towards the glass, her stare momentarily vacant.

Colin gave her a minute, before asking: 'Do you think any of the others are capable of killing Margaret and stealing the necklace?'

He got to his feet while speaking. Their chat felt like it was coming to a natural end, and he was keen to get back to the warmth of the hotel.

'Yes,' she said. 'Like I said, Gavin beat a man half to death. His job prospects aren't exactly rosy, so I imagine a valuable necklace might come in handy for him. Dave is going to have loan sharks at his door soon. I can still picture the pound signs in his eyes when Gavin pointed the necklace out yesterday. And Keith? I don't know about him, but, he really was furious last night. People do crazy things when they're not thinking straight. Chuck in a load of booze and it's a bad mix.'

'Speaking of booze,' Colin said. 'You've taken your cat outfit off.'

'A woman died. You think I'm interested in some loser bet? I'd rather show my respects.'

Colin nodded to the door, but Sophie shook her head.

'I'm going to stay here a while. That hotel, man. The body.' She shivered. 'I'm going to spend as little time as I possibly can there.'

Colin nodded, thanked her for her time and left.

AT THE SAME moment as Colin asked his first question, inside the hotel, Adam's attention was pulled from the television by something moving outside.

Something white was making its way along the path. At first, Adam thought it was one of the presenters, but when he ran through their costumes, a ghost was not among them.

He looked outside again. The figure was definitely draped in white sheets, and a black belt was fastened around the midsection.

And then it hit him.

The figure *was* definitely draped in white sheets, but the belt was not a belt. It was a pair of hands, clasped around the spectre's waist.

Though, spectre was not the right word. Spectres aren't made of flesh and blood.

All at once, Adam realised that Margaret Fernsby's body was below the sheets. And was being moved against her will.

Adam pushed himself off the bed, grabbed his coat and sprinted to the door.

14

RESTING PLACE

ADAM PULLED THE door back and dashed outside, dressed in black with his hood up. He ran up the path, following the invisible footsteps left by whoever was transporting Margaret to pastures new.

When the path split, he hesitated. He could've played a quick game of eenie meenie miney moe and decided his fate that way, but a better idea sprang into mind.

He glanced left at the dense gathering of trees, at the perfect cover their thick trunks provided. He took one last look up the paths, saw that he was alone and ducked into the copse. He leaned his back against the trunk of a particularly large oak tree and waited for his breath to come back. Huge droplets of rain crashed from overhanging leaves, though since he was already soaked through, they made little difference.

After a few minutes, he heard movement. He could feel his heart thump against his chest as he willed himself to take a peek. He summoned the courage, took a final breath and poked his head out.

His cocked an eyebrow as he recognised the familiar gait of the traveller. Cupping his hand to his mouth, he proceeded to imitate the call of a bird. Quite well, if he did say so himself.

When the figure looked over, Adam waved a finger and Colin left the path, joining him behind the oak.

'What was that?' Colin asked. 'You scared the life out of me.'

'It was a wood pigeon's call.'

'More like the call of a strangled cat, you moron.'

'I didn't realise I was on the island with Bill Oddie,' Adam said. 'Anyway, enough about bloody nature, I thought you were talking to Sophie?'

'I was. We went to the chapel. Her idea. Said she couldn't be in the hotel knowing that the body was in there.'

'I think her problem has been solved,' Adam said, before going on to explain what he saw.

'Jesus,' Colin said, once the story of the moving body was finished. 'What do we do?'

'We wait. I figure that whoever is moving her will come back this way. It's the only path back to the hotel.'

And that is what they did.

With only the thick trunks, the bare branches and the darkness for protection from the weather and a conniving killer, they stood and kept watch, daring every so often to flick their heads out either side when they thought they'd heard something. To a casual observer, they may have looked like the most cautious meerkats in existence.

Adam was losing hope and was about to suggest abandoning their post, when he heard something. He looked at Colin, who was looking right back at him with wide eyes.

Adam nodded his head at Colin, who shook his and nodded back.

'Why me?' Adam mouthed.

'Why not?' Colin mouthed back.

With no good argument, Adam very slowly peered around the tree trunk, with fortuitous timing.

Emerging from the right-hand path was a tall figure, dressed from head to toe in black. The black gloves covered hands that swung at the end of long arms.

Adam watched the figure lope past them, eager by the looks of it to get back to the relative safety of the hotel. When he was sure the figure was too far away to hear them, Adam pulled back into the safety of the treeline.

'Well?' Colin whispered.

'Damien,' Adam replied, his voice shaky.

ONCE THE INFORMATION had washed over them, they formed a plan, which they were currently putting into practice.

When they were sure that Damien was happily ensconced in the hotel, Adam and Colin leapt from the treeline and ran up the right-hand path from where Damien had emerged. Chances were that he had dumped the body somewhere along this way.

All Colin and Adam had to do was find it and keep its whereabouts a secret until the police arrived. Presumably, the police would find it anyway when they combed the island on their arrival, but holding up a neon sign for them would be a time-saving and helpful step, evidence-wise.

They made their way up the path, Adam keeping an eye on the trees to the left, Colin the right. They were sure that the body would be buried deep within the wooded area, but a quick sweep now might save them time in the long run.

They arrived at the end of the path no wiser to the body's location. The view from the cliff top, where the path had led them, should've offered a stunning vista—endless ocean, unbroken sky and, on a good day, the rocky beginnings of Scotland. Today, all they got was a solid wall of grey.

'He could've thrown the body over the edge,' Colin said, pointing to the sheer drop below them.

'I don't fancy getting close enough to check,' Adam replied.

The grassy verge was slick with rainfall. One wrong foot placement and you could easily meet your maker on the jagged rocks below.

'We can assume that that's what happened if we don't find it back there,' Colin said, jerking his head in the direction of the woods that they'd just passed through.

They turned and were once again swallowed by the ancient trees on either side. They quickly cooked up a plan—they'd each take a side and venture in to the darkness. If one of them found the body, they'd shout as loudly as they could and hope that they could be heard over the wind.

They were about to split up when Colin saw something that rendered their plan unnecessary.

On his side, about twenty feet into the woods and nearly obscured by the trunks and weather, he could just make out a circular wall of crumbling bricks. Damien had even pointed it out to them on their tour last night.

Was that his plan all along? Nonchalantly point out his planned burial place? Had he dreamed about it on every tour he'd ever given, and finally the urge had smothered him—the sight of the expensive necklace too seductive to ignore?

Colin and Adam crept through the trees, pausing every time one of them stepped on a twig that snapped with the sound of a gun firing. An ominous sound if there ever was one.

When they got to the well, they each took a deep breath and Adam counted down from three with his fingers. When all he was left with was a balled fist, they looked over the top of the crumbling foundations.

And there she was.

Stained blankets covered the bottom of the narrow shaft, dirt accumulating on the sheets and mingling with the dried blood already present.

Underneath what Adam guessed were her feet, lay a long blade, the handle obscured. Blood coated the metal, a mixture of the deceased's and the lucky survivor. Though, Adam doubted if Albert would consider himself lucky. Losing your wife and an expensive necklace, as well as sustaining a significant injury yourself was hardly a day of the blessed.

'What do we do now?' Adam asked, once he was sure that the vomit he felt rising would not be making an appearance the moment he opened his mouth.

'I think we should let the police know what we've found.'

'They're not going to be happy that we've been digging around again. DI Whitelaw isn't exactly our biggest fan after making him look stupid on his last few cases.'

'We could phone Daz?'

Darren was a member of the PSNI and crucially, their friend. They could call him off the clock and have an unofficial chat. In return, he could use this information himself down the line and reap the rewards of Adam and Colin's hard work. It was a symbiotic relationship that had worked well in the past.

'Calling Daz is a good shout,' Adam nodded. 'I've got something I'd like to ask him to check out, too.'

'What?'

Adam prodded the tip of his nose twice with a frozen finger.

'I'd like to keep that to myself for now. It's a hunch, and might be nothing. You go talk to Keith, like we'd planned, and I'll have a chat with Daz.'

They left poor Margaret in her makeshift grave, and trudged back to the house, tired and wet.

THE MAN AT the front desk gave Adam permission to use the landline, before leaving so that he could have whatever conversation was to follow in private.

He found Daz's name in his mobile, copied the number onto the oversized buttons of the hotel's phone and pocketed his iPhone as ringing sounded from the handset pressed to his ear. After a few rings, Darren answered.

His chirpy tone disappeared as Adam launched into the story of murder, theft and his and Colin's subsequent investigation. When he was finished, Darren sounded annoyed.

'Why did you have to get involved? Again?' he asked.

Adam had no good answer to that question, so remained silent while Darren told him that he had done enough; that if he'd seen Damien walking away from where the body had been hidden, then that was a good start for the police when they arrived. He made it very clear, once more, that any further enquiries Colin and Adam felt they needed to conduct should not take place.

Adam confirmed that he understood, aware that Colin was talking to Keith upstairs at that very moment. Technically, the questioning of the Bowie-wannabe was already happening, so didn't fall under Darren's red tape jurisdiction.

'Before you go,' Adam said. 'Can you do me one favour?'

Adam explained said favour. It was met with a sigh.

'What did I just say about you investigating?'

'It wouldn't be me,' Adam said. 'It would be you. It might be nothing and it might be something, and if it is something, think of the kudos you'll get.'

He could hear his friend weigh it up on the other side of the phone. A moment later, the scales tipped in Adam's favour.

'Okay, I'll see what I can do,' Darren said. 'Forecast says the storm should pass by this evening, so we should be there by 8 o'clock or so.'

They bade each other goodbye, Daz reaffirming one final time they should put any Sherlockian tendencies on ice, and as Adam set the phone down, something in the corner of the room moved, making him jump.

'Sorry, mate,' Damien said, emerging like a shadow. 'Didn't mean to startle you.'

'You didn't,' Adam said, shrugging nonchalantly, though not quite pulling it off. He was panicking—how much of his conversation had the weirdo heard?

He reminded Adam of Johnny Depp's strange portrayal of Willy Wonka. The top hat, the velvet coat that hung to his calves, the crazy eyes.

'This is all very exciting,' Damien said. 'A real-life murder mystery.'

'I'd say tragic, rather than exciting.'

'Tomato, tomato. I hear you've been asking a few questions.'

'A few,' Adam agreed.

'You've not been to see me. Is that a good sign or a bad sign?'

'Good, I'd say. You've not aroused our suspicion. I can ask you a few questions now if it would make you feel better?'

'Please do,' Damien said, sitting on one of the plush chairs the spacious reception had to offer. He crossed his legs and adopted an innocent look, fluttering his long eyelashes.

'Did you see anything suspicious last night?'

'Nope. I stayed a while at their party, though it was lame, so I went to my room. Though, I see a lot of different groups coming through here, and these people are unstable. Did you see how they reacted to getting canned?'

'Wouldn't you say anger is normal?'

'Anger, yes. But berating a poor old man and telling him to sell a family heirloom? A bit much if you ask me.'

'Heirloom?'

'The necklace. I was chatting to Albert earlier today— popped in to offer my condolences. He was cut up about having to close the station, and even more upset that they couldn't see the sentimental value of the diamonds. It's been in his family for generations.'

'And he has no idea who took it?'

'No. Do you?'

'We're working on it. Where have you been today?'

'Why?' Damien asked, mock hurt in his features. 'You don't think I have anything to do with this?'

'Not at all,' Adam lied. 'It's just, you're soaking wet.'

'Oh, that. I went down to the boat to make sure it was still there and not damaged. Part of my duties. Dreadful storm,' he said, looking up as if the dark clouds were visible through the ceiling. 'Luckily, it's to die down soon.'

'And the boat is okay?'

'Ah, yeah,' he answered, waving a hand and shrugging, as if he didn't actually know.

'Well, thank you for your time,' Adam said, before making his excuses and leaving Damien dripping on the checkerboard flooring.

15

STARRMAN

TECHNICALLY, COLIN MCLAUGHLIN was flying without a licence. He'd nipped back to his room to change out of his sopping wet clothes and grab a quick snack, so therefore hadn't begun his questioning of Keith when Darren's instruction to cease and desist was ordered.

If life were a television drama, there'd be repercussions. As it was, our newly-clothed, recently replenished, and blissfully unaware amateur investigator walked down the hallway, unbound by law or order. When he reached Keith's door, he raised a hand but did not knock, for a sound on the other side of the divide acted as a pause button.

If anyone happened to come across Colin now, it would look like he was frozen in some sort of political stance; standing straight backed, fist raised against some unknown oppression, to which he was lending his silent support.

In fact, he was trying to make out what the sound was. Initially, it sounded like a vacuum cleaner with a broken fuse which caused the suction to start and stop every few seconds. He realised, quite quickly, that it was in fact Keith snoring.

Sounds like a deviated septum to me, thought Colin, as he hammered on the door, feeling a twinge of guilt in the process.

The strange whirring gave way to a bewildered shout, as Keith was pulled cruelly from his slumber. If time were not of the essence, Colin would perhaps have been kinder. As it was, they needed to hear what Keith had to say.

Heavy footsteps heralded Keith's progress across the room, and when the door was pulled back, Colin could easily imagine him as the faceless killer.

Dark rings surrounded his eyes and a few days' worth of growth clung to his jaw. He was still wearing his sequinned catsuit, though it was not quite as pristine as when he stepped onto the boat less than twenty-four hours ago.

He stared at Colin with a simmering rage.

'What?' he barked.

'I was wondering if I could have a quick chat?'

'I heard Sherlock Holmes was wandering the building.'

'Usually I'm considered the Watson character,' Colin said, hoping to soften Keith's expression with a self-effacing barb.

It didn't work. Keith's jaw remained set and rigid; his unblinking stare fixed on the bridge of Colin's nose. Eventually, he took a step back and motioned for Colin to follow him into the room.

'You woke me up, you know?' Keith asked, as he flopped down on the bed again.

'Sorry about that. I won't keep you long.'

'Get to the point, then.'

Colin watched as he unscrewed a bottle of water and poured it into a glass with smeared fingerprints covering it like graffiti. He took a series of loud gulps before turning his gaze back to Colin.

'You've known Albert a long time, right?'

'Yes,' Keith nodded. 'I've worked at that station for thirty years. Knew his father before him, and Albert has been a close friend for most of my life.'

'And you've been prime-time host for how long?'

'Oh, going on fifteen years now. I'm a very lucky man.'

'We spoke to Sophie earlier...' Colin started, and then stopped, noting Keith's expression. It was as if the mere mention of her name had caused the rainclouds from outside to drift through the window and plant themselves above his head. His cheeks reddened and his brow furrowed.

'I imagine that was a very illuminating chat,' he scoffed.

'Well, she told us about how you were being demoted.'

'Demoted? Is that what she said? Ha, the cheek of the woman. Honestly...' he said, before stopping, as if searching for the words that needed to follow. 'That woman has been nothing but trouble since she turned up.'

'How so?'

'Well, she came in on her first day with an ego—bear in mind she hadn't spoken a single word into the microphone at this stage. I took an instant dislike to her. After her first show, we gathered for cake to celebrate her debut broadcast. I looked across at her at one stage and she was staring at me like... like a witch from a fairy tale. Like she was letting me know she was coming for my job.'

'And she got it.'

'Yep. Didn't take her long once she turned on the charm with Albert.'

'Surely that's not the only reason she got the slot,' Colin said. 'You have to be good at what you do.'

'It helps to be good at what you do, of course, but you want to have seen the two of them round the station. A flirty comment here, a low-cut top there, a friendly hand on the knee in the break room. It was obvious she was using her womanly charms on Albert for her own benefit.'

Colin doubted that a man approaching retirement would be taken in by Sophie's charms, if indeed that was what she was doing.

'And what did Albert do?' he asked, in spite of himself.

'Well, he's a man, isn't he? An old man, but still a red-blooded male. He looked delighted at the attention. It wasn't long until he pulled me into his office and said that the station needed a shake up and that he was considering switching shows. I assumed I was safe...'

'But you weren't?'

'I thought I was, until last night when that harlot told me that she'd been promised my show.'

'And how did you take it?'

'Not well, especially hearing it from her. Vindictive cow. And when you think of all the help I've given him over the years.'

'Help?'

'Albert is notoriously bad with money. His father left him the business in good standing, but Albert made poor investment after poor investment. He's had to take out loans over the years, and then more loans to pay back the loans—that's how bad of a position he's been in. I've waived my salary for a few months to help him out here and there, but that all gets forgotten when a pretty blonde with an agenda turns up.'

'Is he okay now, money-wise?'

'No idea. I stopped taking an interest in anything to do with him. I'd stop turning up for work if it wasn't for my loyal listeners.'

He launched into another tirade against Albert, though Colin was only half-listening. From his tone, it felt like he had been waiting for an age to let this vitriol spill out into the world. Colin's attention was taken by these new revelations of lost money and poor investments.

Could this have something to do with Margaret's death?

When Keith had finished his lengthy diatribe, he leant back against the headboard, breathing heavily like a bull. His belly rose and fell, straining the fabric of his cheap jumpsuit.

'Were Albert and Margaret happy?'

'Yeah,' Keith nodded. 'They've been happily married for nearly forty years. When he had his car accident, she waited on him hand and foot. And I don't mean that in a jokey way, because he only had one foot after the crash.'

He may not have meant it as a joke, but he sure was pleased with it anyway, judging by the silly grin he was attempting to chase away.

'Who do you think killed Margaret?' Colin asked as he stood.

'No idea, I rather think that it's the police's job to find out,' Keith answered, giving Colin a look that suggested it would be an opinion best shared.

'You've been very helpful,' Colin said, taking a few steps towards the door. He reached for the handle, but spun around before taking it in his hand. 'Oh, one last thing.'

Keith nodded.

'Why did you tell Albert to move Margaret's body?'

'I didn't *tell* him to do anything,' Keith scoffed. 'I went to see him, to check how he was doing. The poor man was sitting on the bed, holding on to her cold hand. I suggested to him that he could do with some rest, and maybe having Margaret's body temporarily removed from the room would be for the best. As much as he's screwed me over, I still care for the old codger, in spite of it all.'

'And you didn't think about what the police would say?' Colin asked.

'Like I said, I still care for him. To hell with the fuzz.'

Keith sunk back onto his bed, keen to get a bit more shuteye in, and Colin left him to it.

16

EVIDENCE

FROM OUTSIDE THE bedroom window, it looked like two figures were locked in some sort of passionate Latin dance. Their silhouettes moved past each other, stopping suddenly, before moving back to their original position. Occasionally, one raised an arm.

If you were able to make your way inside and put your eye to the keyhole of room number 9, you'd realise that no rhythmic movement was occurring at all. In fact, the air was not thick with desire; rather, it was teeming with frustration.

'What are you doing?' asked Adam.

'Thinking,' replied Colin.

'Can't you do it sitting down?'

'Why?'

'Because we can't both be pacing up and down. It feels silly.'

Colin gave him a world-wearied sigh, but acquiesced to his request. The floor was now all Adam's, and boy did he intend to use it.

'Right,' he said. 'Where are we?'

'We've had a chat with everyone, and there seems to be no clear standout suspect—any one of them had reason to steal the necklace.'

He ran through the suspects, counting each on a finger.

Ex-prisoner Gavin, debt-riddled Dave, aggrieved-at-having-her-new-prime-time-slot-axed Sophie, and aggrieved-at-having-*his*-old-prime-time-slot-taken-off-him Keith.

'Don't forget Damien. We saw that freak actually walking away from the body.'

'Well, we saw him walk away from that general direction. The boat's captain backed up his story that he had been down at the jetty. He has a solid alibi.'

'Yeah, but, he is a freak, isn't he? He probably could have dumped the body and then turned into a bat and flown down to the dock.'

'Again,' Colin said. 'Let's stick to the realms of possibility.'

'I'll stick to your mum's realms of possibility.'

Colin let the immature comment go, before mentally turning back to the suspect list.

'What we need is evidence,' he said. 'The police have told us we're not allowed to go snooping in their rooms, in case we contaminate it for the forensic team.'

'Whoever's got the firefly necklace is unlikely to be keeping it in their room though, are they? Police turn up, find it straight away and that person is quickly arrested. No, if there were smart, it'd be hidden away somewhere on the island. They'd go and collect it just before the boat departs and dance off into the sunset.'

They both considered the places where it could be hidden for a moment, before Adam once again broke the silence.

'We're discounting one person here.'

'Who?'

'Albert.'

'Come on,' Colin laughed. 'The man's wife has been killed, he's lucky to have escaped with his life, too. Did you see how deep the gash on his arm was? And it's his necklace that's missing. His fortune. There's no need for him to steal it. And, if you need another reason, *he's* the one that asked *us* to investigate.'

'That's not true. You offered and he kinda agreed.'

'Well, he authorised it then, if we're getting into semantics.'

'I still think it's worth a look. He could've been playing us the whole day.'

'I guess it can't hurt to see the full deck of cards,' Colin agreed, somewhat reluctantly. 'But, we can't just go waltzing in to his room, telling him that he is on our list.'

'I've been thinking about this. We've heard his side of the story, but it would be good to have a look around his room, unsupervised. You offer to take him down for a coffee, and I'll hang back and have a nosey.'

'I don't like this,' Colin said.

'Me either, but it's where we are.'

ALBERT OPENED THE door, looking as tired as anyone had ever been. His eyes were red and bloodshot, and his chin quivered. It appeared as if they had caught him mid-cry.

The boys apologised for disturbing him, though he waved it away. He asked them for a moment while he pulled himself together, and closed the door lightly. They heard him muttering to himself and then blowing his nose and a minute later the door reopened.

'What can I do for you?' he said.

'I was wondering if you fancied some company,' Colin replied. 'I thought maybe I could buy you a coffee before dinner?'

'I don't know...'

'Come on. It'll be good for you to get out of the room and have a change of scenery.'

'I suppose,' the old man shrugged. 'It would be nice to go and sit with Margaret for a while, too.'

Colin shot a look at Adam, who simply nodded his head at Albert.

'That would be nice,' he said.

'Are you coming?' Albert asked, as he moved from his room into the corridor.

'Yeah,' Adam nodded.

Albert let go of the door and it began to swing closed. The three of them set off down the hallway and, when they were half way down the stairs, Adam feigned needing the toilet and ran back up the stairs. When he reached Albert's room, he shot a glance back the way he came, but he was alone.

When the old man had been blowing his nose, Adam had bent down and set his wallet against the inside frame of the door. It was dark and blended in with the carpet, so the old man hadn't noticed.

He stooped to pick it up and the closed the door behind him.

He surveyed the room and summoned all of his method acting skills, attempting to become more Daniel Day Lewis than he'd ever been.

If he were a diamond necklace, where would he be?

That's the insane thought that whirled around his head as he moved to the bedside table and pulled drawers out. In them, he found a well-thumbed Bible and a notepad, inside which no grand murder-slash-robbery scheme was written down.

Not that he had expected there to be, but something convenient like that *would* be nice once in a while. It would certainly save him a lot of leg work.

Once finished by the bedside, he got on his hands and knees and looked under the bed. Again, nothing of note.

He crawled around the rest of the room in the same position, hoping his lowly vantage might change the odds. He moved around like a sniffer dog, until he realised how silly this would look to an observer, and was about to push himself up when a sharp pain ripped through his body.

Grimacing, he stood and pulled up his trouser leg. He found the culprit; a thin wedge of glass had embedded itself in his knee. Thankfully, it was only a small shard and pulling it out wasn't too painful.

He went to the bathroom and unwound a large amount of toilet roll. He put the glass in the centre of the pile and wrapped the paper safely around the small shard, before pocketing it. The last thing he needed was the police finding the glass shaving with his blood on it on the floor.

Which, come to think of it, was quite empty.

The police had instructed the hotel staff and the guests not to clean up – to leave everything as it was. Obviously, Albert and Keith had disobeyed that already when they had decided to move the body, though, of course, a compassionate soul may see that as a reasonable thing to do.

But, had someone also swept up the glass? Adam cast an eye over what little glass remained on the floor and windowsill. He wondered if there had been such a pitiful amount when he had been here earlier in the day.

He looked again at the smashed pane, the placement of the handle to open the window, and again at the floor. Surely, a pane that size contained more glass than was currently strewn across the floor. He was about to look outside, when a knock on the door disturbed him.

Adam flattened himself comically against the wall like a mime artist might.

'Albert, are you in there?' a female voice said.

Another knock. And then another.

'We need to talk,' she said, before knocking one more time, and then seemingly giving up, as the knocking and talking stopped.

If this were a novel, Adam perhaps might've realised that he'd been holding his breath the whole time. As it was, his respiratory system had carried on as normal, collecting oxygen without his explicit command.

What he did do was flop to the ground and thank his lucky stars that she hadn't tried to turn the handle. He would've been caught red handed.

And then he saw it. Or rather, he saw something that turned out to be it.

He picked himself up off the floor, hurried across the room and retrieved the piece of paper that was sticking out of Albert's coat's inside pocket. He unfolded it and read it, before reading it again to make sure it was real. He pulled his phone out and snapped a few pictures, before folding the page again and putting it back where he found it.

It may not have been the necklace, but it was close to being the next best thing.

He cast one more glance around and headed for the door.

17

LAID BARE

ADAM HAD JUST finished his speech, detailing his plan of how best to go about not only announcing the killer, but unearthing the necklace too. Colin was still shaking his head a minute later.

'You don't think it's a good idea?' Adam asked, sensing his friend's reticence.

'Even your man-bun seems like a good idea compared to the one you've just told me.'

'What's wrong with it?'

'It went out of fashion a few years ago, it looks greasy, it...'

'The plan, ye numpty,' Adam interrupted. 'Not my hair.'

'Oh. Well, where do I start? For one, we don't have definite proof. It's like a badly done join-the-dots at this stage. Two, if you want us to go through with what you're suggesting and we're wrong, it's going to look like something from a Channel 5 blooper show.'

'And if we're right?'

'It's still not going to look great, is it?'

'So what?' Adam asked. 'If he gets hurt, it's something he should've thought about before killing an old lady and stealing her necklace. Also, we do have proof. I've shown you what I've got and you've kind've confirmed it with what you got.'

Colin considered this for a while.

'I guess you're right. The evidence does sort of point to them, doesn't it? And if we're wrong, screw it. We don't have to see these people again.'

They high-fived and Adam got to work on his computer. It didn't take long to achieve what he had set out to do. When he was finished, he sat back on his chair with a satisfied sigh and pulled his backpack towards him. He fished around inside it without looking, searching for a snack, when his fingers touched something he hadn't realised was in there.

It would probably come in handy, he thought, though the torment that Colin would bestow upon him afterwards might not be worth it. Quick as a flash, he pulled the item in question out and stuffed it into his back pocket, just as his friend came out of the bathroom.

Adam checked his watch. It was almost time for dinner, which would mean that the assembled cast would all be gathering around the table soon. They ran through the plan quickly one last time, before Adam scooped his laptop up and they left the room together.

It was show time.

THE DINING ROOM had a more subdued air than the last time they'd all been here together. The good humour and convivial atmosphere had been stripped away, replaced instead with an impression of suspicion and wariness. Though tragedy had occurred, the smell of a roast dinner wafting through the corridors had beckoned everyone to the same room.

Alongside Colin and Adam, Gavin, Dave, Sophie and Keith now sat around the huge table, though none were talking. Each sat, as if forced to be here, their eyes on the door to the kitchen, in the hope that food would soon appear, so that they could eat and depart to the solitude and relative safety of their rooms.

As Colin and Adam had passed Albert's room, the old man had poked his head out and asked Colin to bring his food up to the bedroom as he couldn't bear to be in the same room as a murdering thief. In the end, they'd managed to convince him to come down with them, with a promise that they wouldn't let any further hurt occur.

Back in the room, Colin gave Adam a look. Now that they were here, in the presence of their suspected killer, the plan seemed less watertight to Adam than before. The words he'd spoken, and the certainty with which he had drummed them home, now seemed empty and untrustworthy in company.

However, he hadn't made a PowerPoint presentation for nothing. Also, the storm was beginning to subside and he wanted the credit for catching the baddie, rather than doing all the legwork just for the police to walk away with the kudos.

He stood, and all eyes moved to him.

'I've prepared a little something that I'd like to share with you all,' he said. 'In light of the station closing down, consider this a walk through time.'

He crossed the room and stroked his finger over the mousepad of the computer, which caused the screen to light up and the projector's beam to awaken. On the fabric screen was the beginning of the presentation. It showed a black and white picture of the station, which he had lifted directly from the presentation from the night before.

In fact, he'd lifted most of it from the presentation Albert had shown the night before. As the pages rolled on, groans sounded from the table.

Adam paused the slideshow.

'Okay,' he said. 'I realise it's very similar to the one you saw last night, but there's one almighty difference that I'm sure all of you will be very pleased to see. Well, almost everyone.'

Adam turned to Albert.

'Mr Fernsby, please could you join me?'

The old man shot him a quizzical look and then pushed himself up, before hobbling across the room to join Adam on the dancefloor.

'Albert, we've found out who killed your wife and stole the expensive firefly necklace.'

'Who?' he gasped.

The silence in the room seemed to swell, just as the slide that wasn't in last night's presentation appeared on the screen. Everyone's attention shifted to it as Adam pressed the freeze button to keep it locked in place.

'You can give up the act now,' Adam said.

'PREPOSTEROUS!' ALBERT SHOUTED, taking two steps back from Adam. 'Absolutely preposterous. My wife dies. No, not dies, is murdered, and a precious family heirloom stolen and you have the audacity to finger me?'

'Less of the drama,' Adam replied, quietly.

Colin's time to shine was about to arrive. He still couldn't believe what he was about to do. While silent chaos reigned, he got out of his seat, tiptoed across the dancefloor and got down on his hands and knees behind the old man.

He gave Adam a nod, and his friend did the rest.

ADAM NOTED COLIN'S nod and knew that it was his time to act. This part of the plan had seemed cool in theory, but now that he was in the here and now, it seemed kind of cruel.

Still, Colin was clearly committed so he would look stupid if he didn't hold up his end of the bargain.

With surprising speed, he closed the distance between himself and the old man, and shoved him in the chest with as much force as he could muster.

For a second, time seemed to slow. Adam felt the old man's bony ribs and registered the look of surprise on his face. He heard the shouts of the presenters, though they seemed a million miles away.

When time caught up with itself, he watched Albert topple over Colin's kneeling body and collide painfully with the floor. Adam had been subjected to this humiliation on the school's grounds many a time. It hurt your pride more than your body. But only just.

'What the…' Albert wheezed.

Adam held a finger across his own lips to silence the old man, before turning to the presenters who looked like they were about to stand up for their felled ex-boss.

'He's the killer and the thief,' he said, triumphantly. 'And here's the proof.'

Adam strode around the room, milking the moment. He heard Colin cough and, when Adam looked at his friend, he was giving him the "get on with it" look that he'd perfected over the years.

'Okay, here we go. Firstly, the crime scene. Why, I ask you, would a supposedly exhausted woman who wanted to go to bed need a sleeping tablet? I'll tell you why. Albert slipped it in her water to make sure she would drift off nice and quickly. And then he killed her. There never was anyone else in the room. He killed his wife and knifed himself to make it look like he'd been attacked too.'

'What about the knife?' Keith asked.

'Well, after he'd finished being stabby-stabby, he smashed the window and threw it outside. You see, generally glass falls in the direction it's pushed, and there wasn't much on the carpet but there was loads outside. Also, the ivy on the trellis outside his room hadn't been disturbed at all. That was his first silly mistake.'

'What was his second?'

Adam pointed at the screen. On it was a picture of the piece of paper he'd found in Albert's safe.

'I present to you exhibit number two. And this really shows the man's stupidity. This is a picture of a letter from his insurers, with whom he recently took out a policy for, you guessed it, a rather expensive necklace to cover damage and, you guessed it again, theft.'

He held his tongue for a while, giving everyone a chance to take in the contents of the letter and the eye-wateringly large sum of money Albert was in line to claim.

'Of course,' Adam continued, when he figured he had milked the moment long enough. 'There might be one or two questions asked from the insurers when they cotton on to the policy being taken out very recently. What are the odds?'

'This is all nonsense,' Albert muttered. 'I took the policy out not long after getting the firefly necklace valued. I hadn't realised the amount of money that it was worth. I have the valuers report, dated a day before the new policy was taken out.'

'Convenient, and very clever,' Adam said. And he *did* look impressed. 'And, of course, someone might buy that excuse if it weren't for the fact you had an accomplice lined up to help you clear away your mess once you got here.'

A gasp went up around the room, as the presenters eyed each other with suspicion.

'Sophie Saunders,' Adam said. 'She was your right-hand man, wasn't she?'

Sophie began to deny it, but was cut off by Albert.

'How did you know?'

It was the old man's turn to look impressed.

'I'm glad you asked. Well, we figured you had help shifting the knife from outside your room when you'd dropped it through the window. When we got to thinking, there were a number of reasons.' He turned to Sophie. 'Firstly, your co-workers aren't all that impressed with your presenting ability. Fine for mid-morning drivel, but prime-time? Nah. So, there must've been another reason for your promotion.'

'Sex,' laughed Gavin, looking at Albert. 'At your age? You filthy old…'

'As much as it pains me to imagine it,' Adam interrupted, 'yes. But it wasn't just sex, was it? It was blackmail. You gave him a bit of the good stuff on the mainland and then you concocted the plan to kill off poor Margaret.'

'You were telling him in plain sight that he best not back out at the dinner last night. You were talking about love and threatening to expose who it was, but he cut you off,' Colin said, failing to look serious with the old man's legs still draped over his back.

'It was all her idea,' Albert said.

'Shut up,' Sophie shouted, and attempted to run out of the room. Gavin leapt up from his seat and caught her with his impossibly long arms.

'So, if these two are guilty, where is the necklace?' Keith asked.

This was the part Adam had been dreading, though his pride at throwing three darts and landing them all had increased his confidence. He marched across the floor and took Albert's prosthetic leg in his hand.

He looked the old man in the eye and yanked.

Adam realised how this must look. He could feel every eye on him. He tipped the hollow leg, and felt something move inside it. He angled it further and watched as the necklace tipped out, onto the wooden floor.

The purple firefly and diamonds glittered in the light.

'Busted,' Adam said, and swooped down on the old man. He slipped one of the handcuffs around Albert's wrists and motioned for Gavin to bring Sophie over. He cuffed her too.

Everyone stepped back to take in the defeated couple. Their attention was not fixed on the two criminals, per se. Rather, what was holding them together.

After an awkward moment, Colin spoke.

'What the hell are those?'

'Handcuffs,' Adam answered quietly, his face growing red.

'I can see that. Pink, fluffy handcuffs. Why do you have them?'

Adam glanced around to find the groups undivided attention fixed on him.

'Well, Helena and I, we...'

Damien chose the perfect moment to enter the room, the police trailing after him. He'd been waiting by the jetty for their arrival ever since the worst of the rain had stopped.

Detective Inspector Whitelaw stepped past the tour guide.

'What are those?' he asked.

Adam's burning face grew even redder.

18

ALL'S WELL THAT ENDS WELL

HELENA SET HER fork on the plate with a clatter and leaned back, rubbing her belly appreciatively. Adam's cooking had really come along in the past few months.

'And then what?' she asked.

He'd been telling her all about his crazy weekend.

The necklace.

The death.

Damien.

Although, in the aftermath of the police carting Albert and Sophie away, Adam and Colin had spent some time with Damien. He had, after all, played a small part in their plan by leading the police swiftly to the theatre of conflict.

They'd had a few beers together and underneath his creepy persona, they'd found a down to earth guy who loved his job. Namely, unsettling the bejesus out of unsuspecting guests. They'd exchanged numbers, and goodbyes had been punctuated by promises of drinks in Stonebridge.

Adam finished his story, stopping short of admitting that he used their handcuffs to apprehend the suspects.

They left their plates on the table and retreated to the sofa. Strictly was just starting, much to Adam's dismay.

'I'm thinking of dying my hair that colour,' Helena said, pointing to a flame-haired dancer. 'But I'm not sure.'

He listened to her weigh up the pros and cons of the dye job, offering his two pence when the opportunity presented itself. The rest of the evening passed in a haze of wine and as the night drew in, Adam's eyes grew heavy.

He suggested going to bed and she threw a suggestive look his way.

Christ, he thought, *I hope she's not expecting to be restrained tonight.*
And with that thought fresh in his mind, he trailed after her,
towards the confines of the bedroom.